SQUAW MOUNTAIN MASSACRE

By Doyle Trent

ZEBRA BOOKS
KENSINGTON PUBLISHING CORP.

ZEBRA BOOKS

are published by

Kensington Publishing Corp.
475 Park Avenue South
New York, NY 10016

Copyright © 1985 by Doyle Trent

All rights reserved. No part of this book may be reproduced in any form or by any means without the prior written consent of the Publisher, excepting brief quotes used in reviews.

First printing: July 1985

Printed in the United States of America

NEAR DEATH

"Mister," McCrea said. A guttural groan came from the man's throat. McCrea touched him on the shoulder and turned him over on his back. It was then that he noticed the feet. The feet were covered with large red blisters. The man had been horribly burned.

Revulsion worked up into McCrea's throat as he took off his duck jacket, folded it and placed it gently under the old man's head. His voice was unsteady when he asked, "What—what happened, mister? Who did this to you?"

Suddenly a bullet screamed off a rock at McCrea's foot. For a second he stood still, unbelieving. But then, just as the next shot was fired, he dove headfirst behind a boulder. "Hey," he yelled, his voice a little out of control. "Hey, what the hell're you doing?" Then he realized his question was stupid. What the shooter was doing was trying to kill him. Why? He didn't know, and this was not the time to lie on his belly and wonder about it. . . .

THE BEST IN WESTERNS FROM ZEBRA

THE SLANTED COLT (1413, $2.25)
by Dan Parkinson
A tall, mysterious stranger named Kichener gave young Benjamin Franklin Black a gift—a Colt pistol that had belonged to Ben's father. And when a cold-blooded killer vowed to put Ben six feet under, it was a sure thing that Ben would have to learn to use that gun—or die!

GUNPOWDER GLORY (1448, $2.50)
by Dan Parkinson
After Jeremy Burke shot down the Sutton boy who killed his pa, it was time to leave town. Not that Burke was afraid of the Suttons—but he had promised his pa, right before the old man died, that he'd never kill another Sutton. But when the bullets started flying, he'd find there was more at stake than his own life....

BLOOD ARROW (1549, $2.50)
by Dan Parkinson
Randall Kerry was a member of the Mellette Expedition—until he returned from a scouting trip to find the force of seventeen men slaughtered and scalped. And before Kerry could ride a mile from the massacre site, two Indians emerged from the trees and charged!

THE LAST MOUNTAIN MAN (1480, $2.25)
by William W. Johnstone
Trouble and death followed Smoke all of his days—days spent avenging the ones he loved. Seeking at first his father's killer, then his wife's, Smoke rides the vengeance trail to find the vicious outlaws—and bring them to his own kind of justice!

GUNSIGHT LODE (1497, $2.25)
by Virgil Hart
After twenty years Aaron Glass is back in Idaho, seeking vengeance on a member of his old gang who once double-crossed him. The hardened trail-rider gets a little softhearted when he discovers how frail Doc Swann's grown—but when the medicine man tries to backshoot him, Glass is tough as nails!

Available wherever paperbacks are sold, or order direct from the Publisher. Send cover price plus 50¢ per copy for mailing and handling to Zebra Books, Dept. 1635, 475 Park Avenue South, New York, N.Y. 10016. DO NOT SEND CASH.

Chapter One

The spiral of smoke rising lazily on the other side of the willow bushes should have been no cause for alarm. But it caused John McCrea to rein up suddenly, eyes narrowed.

Perhaps it was because he didn't expect to see another human around here. The smoke had to be coming from a camp fire.

Or perhaps it was because it brought an angry memory to mind—the memory of another spiral of smoke. And of a dying man.

McCrea sat his slick fork saddle straight up, back stiff. The Diamond J gelding he was riding fidgeted but was glad to stop climbing the high slope for a moment and catch its breath.

The rider's eyes took in the terrain, watching for movement. It was rough country: high, steep, and spotted with ponderosa and lodgepole pine. A towering snowcapped peak to the north looked down on everything. A few small patches of quaking aspen grew on the hillsides and along the creek ahead. The leaves had already turned yellow and were beginning to fall.

McCrea and the other Diamond J riders were combing the high valleys and ridges in the new state of Colorado, catching the cows and calves drifting down from the Continental Divide ahead of winter. But McCrea had seen no cattle that day and had not seen another human since he had left the Diamond J wagons shortly after daybreak. His jaw muscles tensed at the sight of the smoke. It was that memory.

But, he reminded himself, that was in a different part of the country and over a year ago. This had to be another Diamond J rider trying to warm up the cold biscuits and bacon the riders carried for their noon meal.

Slowly, McCrea forced the tension out of his body. Forget the past. Not all smoke meant death and destruction.

Just before he started across the narrow creek he stopped and called out, "Hello."

The fire had to be just on the other side of a line of dense willows, between the willow and a pile of huge granite boulders.

"Hello."

When he got no answer his jaw tightened and his back stiffened again. He wanted to turn the horse around and leave, but that would not do. When a man happened across another man in the high country he had to stop and say hello, or say something.

McCrea tried to be cautious as he rode forward, and he winced at the splashing sounds his horse made fording the creek. Why didn't he get an answer? Who was camped over there?

You can't warm up cold biscuits and bacon.

With a knot of fear in his stomach, McCrea pushed through the willows and rode around the pile of boulders.

What he saw made him rein up suddenly again. His breath caught in his throat.

A crumpled figure of a man lay beside a dying fire, and McCrea could see that the man's hands and feet were tied and his feet were bare.

Fear welled up in McCrea as he stared at the scene. A shiver ran up his back. He felt as though he were being watched, and he looked around cautiously. Finally he yelled "hello" again, hoping the man would stir and warn him of any danger. The man did not move.

"Lordy," McCrea muttered under his breath. "What in hell is going on here?"

He sat his saddle quietly for a long moment, eyes taking in the terrain, the camp, everything. A pair of handsome sorrel mules, one carrying a riding saddle and the other a pack saddle, grazed along the creek. McCrea had to go to the man, see if he was alive and help him if he was. He couldn't just ride away and pretend he had not seen him.

Warily, he rode up to the smouldering fire and dismounted. The man was lying on his side, eyes tightly shut. His mouth inside a bushy grey beard was opening and closing but making no sound. The man was old, wrinkled, nearly bald.

"Mister," McCrea said. A guttural groan came from the man's throat. McCrea touched him on the shoulder and turned him over on his back. It was then that he noticed the feet. The feet were covered with large red blisters. The man had been horribly burned.

Revulsion worked up into McCrea's throat as he took off his duck jacket, folded it and placed it gently under the old man's head. His voice was unsteady when he asked, "What—what happened, mister? Who did this to you?"

Again, the mouth opened and closed inside the beard, and the eyes rolled from side to side. The right hand moved slowly toward the dying camp fire, toward a few groceries, a skillet, a coffeepot, a can of Lidden's condensed milk, an open five-pound bag of Morning Star sugar. Still, only guttural grunts came from the twisting lips. The hand reached the sugar sack and tipped it over, spilling the contents. The fingers of the hand separated, and the index finger pointed to the emptying sack.

"What happened?" McCrea repeated, trying to hold down the bile in his throat. "Who did this to you?"

The eyes squinched tight, the mouth clamped shut, and the old man's breathing became ragged, tortured. The body in worn, faded clothes shuddered in pain. And as McCrea watched, horrified, the face relaxed, the eyes and mouth opened, and the breathing stopped.

McCrea's first impulse was to get on his horse and ride hard back to the Diamond J wagons. The old man was dead. It was murder. It had to be reported to the law.

The law? McCrea had little use for the law. If the law had done its job down there in the New Mexico Territory he would not be a homeless drifter, running from a horrible memory. But he prided himself in being a law-abiding citizen, and this had to be reported.

He stood up and reached for the bridle reins. The sudden movement caused the young, half-broken horse to shy away, dragging the reins, and McCrea had to move fast to grab the end of the left rein before the animal could get away. That's what saved his life.

A bullet screamed off a rock at the same time McCrea heard the shot.

For a second he stood still, unbelieving, then, just as

the next shot was fired, he dove headfirst behind the boulders that had shielded the old man's camp fire. "Hey," he yelled, his voice a little out of control. "Hey, what the hell're you doing?" Then he realized his question was stupid. What the shooter was doing was trying to kill him. Why? Hell, he didn't know, and this was not the time to lie on his belly and wonder about it. Another shot hit the coffeepot and sent it spinning.

McCrea hugged the ground. He tried to figure out where the shots were coming from, but he was afraid to look up. He had to look up. He had to move. He couldn't just lie there and let somebody pump bullets into him. For the first time since he had left the Pecos Valley, McCrea wished he had a gun. Almost everybody but McCrea carried a gun. He had left his old Colts .44-40 in the bottom of his warbag at the wagon. He had once vowed never to carry a gun again. But when he made the vow, he didn't expect to stumble over a dead man in the high country of southern Colorado and get shot at because of it. Without a gun he was helpless.

"Lordy," he muttered to himself. "Dammit anyway." Jaws clamped tight, he raised his head to where he could see over the waist-high boulders. The shooter could be behind any of those big rocks across a small grassy valley. One of the rocks was as big as a small house and was only a hundred yards away.

McCrea saw the puff of smoke and ducked immediately. He heard the bullet whine over his head. Yes, the shooter was on top of that big rock. All that kept him from coming down and shooting McCrea point-blank was the possibility that McCrea had a gun. If he knew what McCrea knew, McCrea would soon be as dead as the old man. He had to get away somehow.

Glancing behind him, McCrea tried to see a way to back off without exposing himself. He would never make it to the horse, that was for certain, and it was a long walk back to the wagons. He decided that walking was better than dying, and he would walk if he could get out of sight of the shooter. While he was searching for an escape route, he saw the rifle.

It was an old one, a long-barreled, lever action gun, and it was propped against a tree across from the camp fire. The once blue barrel was shiny in places, and the stock was bleached from the weather. To get to it, McCrea would have to leave his cover and make a target of himself. Desperate, he studied the terrain again. There was no escape. He had to go for the gun. With the gun he could shoot back. Without it he had no chance at all.

McCrea raised to a squatting position and got his feet under him. The thing to do, he decided, was to grab the rifle on the run and keep running until he got behind that big ponderosa over there. Still squatting, he took off the heavy spurs. He wished he could take off the leather chaps. He had to run as fast as he had ever run in his life, and a man couldn't win a foot race wearing chaps. But he would have to stand up to take them off. He resisted the temptation to look over the boulder he was hiding behind to see if the shooter was watching him. He had to run and he had to do it now.

A bullet ricocheted with a deadly whine off the boulders, and McCrea ran. He leaped over the old man's body, nearly tripped, staggered, kept his balance and ran. Another bullet knocked splinters off the tree where the rifle was as McCrea reached for it. Instinctively, he drew his hand back, then reached for it again, got it and ran.

The big ponderosa had roots as thick as a man's leg,

and McCrea tripped over one of them, fell, and rolled behind the tree. A bullet hit the ground beside him. He got to his knees behind the tree and jacked the lever down on the old rifle. It was a Henry repeater, a .44 caliber, a Civil War Yankee Rifle. It was old but well cared for, and it was loaded. McCrea had to expose his head to see around the tree, to try to spot the shooter. The sound of the next shot made him jerk his head back as splinters from the side of the tree struck him in the face. The bullets were coming from either a small caliber gun or one heavy enough to partially muffle the sound.

The shooter was down beside the biggest boulder now. Or maybe it was a different man. McCrea raised the long barrel, squinted through the open rear sight, put the front sight on the spot where the last shot had come from and squeezed the trigger. The old Henry roared like a cannon and kicked like a mule.

McCrea got a glimpse of a man running. He levered another shell into the firing chamber, took quick aim and fired again. The man disappeared.

Was he hit? Nothing was happening. Was there another man? McCrea was bolder now that the shooting had stopped. He looked from behind the ponderosa and studied the country ahead of him. It was more rough country: steep, rocky, and pine covered. An army could be hidden in those rocks and trees. Eyes strainng, McCrea watched for movement. The only way to spot a living creature in the timber, he had learned, was to watch for movement. That is what he had been told by cowboys who were used to hunting cattle in the mountain country. That is what Judson Olesky had advised him to do when he sent him up this way.

There was no movement. Was the shooter down?

McCrea squinted, afraid to blink, afraid he would miss something. Was it a standoff with the loser being the one who moved first? McCrea saw that his horse, a bay gelding with a Diamond J brand on its left hip, had spooked at the gunfire but had stepped on the reins and was now standing still. It was then that he heard the hoofbeats: the sound of shod hooves clattering over the rocks. The sound came from behind the big boulder across the narrow valley. Someone was leaving.

Five more minutes passed before McCrea decided to take a chance and quit the shelter of the ponderosa. Eyes still searching the terrain, he half ran to the horse, gathered the reins and stepped into the saddle. He carried the Henry across the saddle in front of him as he spun the bay gelding around on its hind feet and headed it downhill as fast as it could pick its way over the rocks.

Chapter Two

Crystal Lee Brown looked through the window of her Bluebird Cafe and watched the rider go past at a gallop on a horse that had run about as far as it could run. She saw the rider try to bring the horse to a stop, then he stepped off easily as the horse went on down the street. She saw the man hesitate, look up at the sheriff's sign over the boardwalk, then go inside the sheriff's office.

Crystal Lee's curiosity was aroused at the way the man had hurried, and she continued watching out the window. She saw Sheriff G.B. Harvey come outside, the man beside him, and turn with hurried steps toward his own stable two blocks up the street. The man paused, looked up and down the main street of Bluebird, Colorado, and let his eyes roam, curiously, at the clapboard buildings and all the new construction going on. He saw the new hotel going up and the courthouse and the bank nearing completion a block down the street.

For a couple of seconds his eyes showed interest when they met hers, then quickly he looked away, seemingly embarrassed.

The man was in his late twenties, a little above average in height, slender but strong looking. He wore the leather stovepipe chaps with a fringe down the sides that most mountain cowboys wore for protection in the buck brush and willows, but he had no spurs on his boots. His black hat was a little out of the ordinary with a curl in the brim and the crown creased in a high square fashion. He had a good face with a strong chin, a wide mouth and intelligent grey eyes.

He shot another glance at Crystal, allowed a small smile to widen his mouth, then turned and followed the sheriff. Soon, the cowboy and the sheriff rode past at a gallop, the sheriff on a buckskin mare and the cowboy on a roan that he had no doubt borrowed from Johnson's Corrals. The cowboy sat on his saddle easily while the sheriff rode hunched over, a harried expression on his face. Something had happened. Something had Sheriff G.B. Harvey worried.

Crystal retied the clean white apron about her slender middle, smoothed it over hips that flared just enough to make it known at a glance that she was a shapely young woman, and went back to the counter. It was mid-afternoon and only one customer sat at the counter, sipping coffee. With a clean cloth, she wiped bread crumbs away from another place on the counter, picked up a dirty plate and a coffee cup and went into the kitchen. Maudie had just finished washing the noon dishes and was opening the back door, preparing to throw out the water from a small tin washtub.

"Take a rest, Maudie," Crystal said. "You look as tired as I feel."

"Yes ma'am," Maudie said. "I shorely could use a rest."

"As soon as I can find somebody, I'll hire more help," Crystal said. "We're both working too hard. Business is too good."

"Yes ma'am." Maudie threw out the dishwater and rinsed the tub with clean water from a bucket. She poured herself a cup of coffee, settled her plump rump in a chair at the work table and put her chin in her black hands. "My pore feet. I'm shorely glad to get off my pore feet for awhile."

"It will be Sunday in a few days and we can both take a rest, Maudie. These miners are just going to have to find someplace else to eat on Sundays."

Sunday was Crystal's favorite day. On Sunday she would go to Johnson's Corrals, saddle the gentle horse Johnson had sold her and ride up into the higher valleys. She would pack some sandwiches and enjoy being alone with her horse and the fall mountain scenery.

Maudie folded her hands and rolled her brown eyes toward Crystal. "You work as hard as I do, Miss Brown, and I'm tard so you must be tard, too. Come Sunday, they can eat at that Palace Saloon. I heard one of 'em say he use to eat there, but he likes your cookin' better."

Crystal Lee Brown smiled a wry smile. "Funny, but a few months ago I would have enjoyed a compliment like that. I needed the business. The ranchers and ranch hands around here don't come to town often enough to keep a cafe busy." She sighed. "But ever since that sheepherder found gold on Willow Creek, men have been pouring into Bluebird from all over the nation, and I just can't feed them fast enough."

She sat at the table, too, and put her white hand on Maudie's black arm. "I don't know what I'd do without you, Maudie. I intend for you to have a share of the profits. You have earned it."

Maudie smiled, strong white teeth gleaming against her dark face. "I don't know what I'd do without you, Miss Brown. You gave me a job after my Charlie fell and hurt his back. We'd of starved if it hadn't been for you."

Crystal sighed again and stood up. "Time to start cutting the meat for supper. You just sit there awhile and finish your coffee."

"You're a nice lady, Miss Brown, I don't care what they said."

"What?" Crystal stopped suddenly and turned back. "Who said? Who said what?"

Maudie fingered a small chip on the rim of her china coffee mug. "He said he knew about you, Miss Brown, but I don't believe him."

"What Maudie?" Crystal faced her hired help, hands on hips. "What did he say?"

"He said he knowed you before. Said he seen you before. Said he seen you workin' in a—" The black woman paused and swallowed a lump in her throat. "A house down in Texas." She looked up at Crystal, eyes tormented. "I don't care what they said, Miss Brown, you're a nice lady."

Crystal Lee Brown's face blanched, and she suddenly felt weak. She dropped into a chair beside Maudie and put her face in her hands. "Oh my God."

The black woman wanted to do something to make her employer feel better. She wrung her hands and finally put an arm around Crystal's shoulders. "Don't you worry, Miss Brown. I ain't repeatin' nothin'. Not even to my Charlie. You're a nice lady, Miss Brown, I don't care what they said."

* * *

Only two men were at the Diamond J wagons when McCrea and Sheriff G.B. Harvey rode up. The wagons, a canvas-covered chuck wagon and an open bed wagon, were spotted on a rocky meadow at the foot of a high timber-covered ridge. Cow boss Judson Olesky drained his coffee cup with a bobbing of his prominent adam's apple, put the cup in a tin wash pan and hitched up his wool pants. He was buggy whip thin, and he wore a drooping moustache and a dirty white flat-brim hat. His striped wool pants were tucked into high-heeled boots with pull leathers that reached halfway down to his spurs.

"Here they come," he said to Fletch, the cook. "No need to put the coffeepot back on the fire. They won't have time to stay."

McCrea and the sheriff rode up at a fast trot on winded horses. Harvey glanced around and asked, "Where's your crew, Jud?"

The sheriff and the cow boss were both middle-aged, but there the similiarity ended. Harvey was clean shaven and stout with thick grey hair and pale blue eyes under heavy grey eyebrows. He also wore wool pants and a white hat, but his pants and hat were clean. A double-action, silver-plated six gun rode high on his right hip.

"Out gatherin' stock," Olesky answered. "I figured you'd need some fresh hosses, and I kept a couple out of the remuda. If that dead man is where I think he is, we'll have to ride to get there before dark. You can put yore mare in that corral yonder if you want to, Harv, and you can throw yore saddle on that stockin'-legged sorrel."

Judson Olesky had his horse saddled and ground hitched fifty feet from the chuck wagon, and he waited until the two men caught and saddled fresh horses and were mounted again, then joined them. "From what you said, John, I think I know where he is, but you better lead the way."

They rode in silence most of the way. The horses kept up a slow gallop until they started the steep climb, then they were allowed to walk.

"You sure you can find him?" Harvey asked.

"He's right between here and all that snow up there." McCrea nodded toward the highest peak in sight. "He's on the other side of a creek."

The sun had slipped over the high, jagged western horizon when the three men rode into the dead man's camp. The body was exactly where McCrea had left it. The coffeepot with a bullet hole in it was still where it had fallen. The spilled sugar had attracted a few ants. "I left his rifle back at the wagon," McCrea said. "I didn't want to pack it to town."

They dismounted. Harvey squatted beside the body and looked it over without touching it. "It's Old Levi." His eyes roved over the dead man and when he saw the feet he swore. "Somebody sure put him through hell before they killed him. Look at that. Damn near burned him alive."

"Why, I remember him," Olesky said. "That's the old sourdough that hung around town last winter, ain't it? Why'd anybody want to kill him?"

"Gold, that's why."

Olesky grunted. "You mean Old Levi struck it rich somewhere?"

"He sure did." The sheriff turned the body over and studied it. "Can't find any bullet holes. He surely would have bled some if he was shot."

"Maybe they beat 'im to death." The ranch foreman squatted beside the sheriff. "He was purty old. Prob'ly wouldn't take much to beat an old man to death."

"He was a tough old bird. He wouldn't give up easy. Could have been heart failure."

McCrea had stood by quietly while the sheriff and Olesky looked over the body. Finally, he spoke. "They had to have sneaked up on him because his rifle was leaning against that quakie over there. They didn't give him a chance to grab it."

"Looks like he was fixing himself a pot of coffee and was eating some bread when they came up on him." Harvey grunted as he stood up. "You don't have to be a wizard to figure out what happened."

"They got the drop on 'im," the ranch foreman said, "tied 'im up and tortured 'im. You say he struck it rich somewhere, Harv?"

"No doubt about it. But," the sheriff said, looking down at the body, a scowl on his face, "it's hard to feel sorry for a killer."

"A killer?" The Diamond J cow boss squinted at Harvey, then said, "Oh yeah. I remember now. He's the one that went up there somewhere with a partner a year or so ago and came back by hisself."

"That's him. He wouldn't talk about it. Wouldn't talk at all. I think he was a little out of his head. But he had a poke of dust that was pure gold. We figure he killed his partner, but we couldn't prove it. We rode and climbed all over that country up there, and we never did find any trace of anything or anybody. Just a hell of a lot of snow."

"Maybe his partner died of a accident. It's easy to get hurt trampin' around in these hills."

"If that's so, why didn't he say so and take us to the body? Or the grave?"

"He didn't say nothin'?"

19

"He wouldn't talk to anybody. He hung around town all winter, spent his dust on booze, and about the end of June he disappeared. Nobody saw him again for a few months until he showed up again a couple weeks ago carrying another poke of dust. And he had his pockets full of nuggets the likes of which nobody around here has ever seen."

"Well," Olesky said, hitching the wool pants up on his skinny frame, "it's clear what happened. Somebody tried to make 'im tell where his strike is."

Harvey squinted at McCrea from under his bushy eyebrows. "He was still alive when you found him?"

"For a few minutes."

"Did he say anything?"

"No. I asked him who did it, and he tried to say something but he couldn't get the words out."

"Did you move him?"

"Well sure. I cut the ropes off him and turned him over on his back. That's my jacket under his head there."

"And he didn't tell you anything?"

"No."

The sheriff continued squinting at McCrea as if he didn't know whether to believe him. Finally, he looked around, eyes searching for something. "He bought two mules a couple of days ago. He must have been riding one and leading one. Wonder where they are."

"They were grazing on the swamp grass along the creek when I left. One was carrying a riding saddle and the other was carrying a cross buck saddle and a pair of panniers. They can't be far away. I'll see if I can find them." McCrea walked to his horse, mounted and rode away.

Harvey glanced at the ranch foreman. "Did I

understand him to say his name is McCrea?"

"Yup. John McCrea."

"I heard that name before somewhere." The sheriff frowned in concentration, then said, "Damn. It's going to be dark in a little while. Wish I had more daylight."

"You can stay at the wagons tonight, shurff. I'll loan you some blankets and a tarp. And I'll send somebody back with you in the mornin' to help pack 'im out."

"Thanks, Jud, but I'll have to get him out of here tonight. You know about rigor mortis, I guess. He'll be damn hard to tie on a horse when he gets stiff. I hope your man finds those mules, especially that one with a pack saddle."

"Whatta you think, Harv? Did somebody make 'im tell where he found gold?"

"I don't know. If your man is telling the truth, he was alive when he found him, and I'd guess that whoever was torturing him wasn't through. Whoever it was probably saw or heard your man coming and took cover."

"Olesky nodded toward the big boulder. "John said he was shot at from on top of that rock over there and again from the ground."

"If that's true, that's what happened then. Too bad your man didn't get here sooner. McCrea, huh?" The sheriff was puzzling over the name when McCrea rode up, leading the two sorrel mules.

They found a small tent tied across the pack saddle and got the body wrapped in it and lashed onto the pack mule, legs on one side and head and shoulders on the other. McCrea found his discarded spurs and buckled them on his boots. It was dark then. Sheriff G.B. Harvey said he would have to ride most of the night getting the body back to town, and then he would have to come right back and search the murder scene again in the daylight.

"If I'd known I was going to have to do all this riding, I wouldn't have been out early this morning prospecting," he said. "Believe me, the governor didn't do me any favors when he made me sheriff."

"You got a mystery on yore hands, shurff. I hope you find out who done it. Whoever he is, he's a mean sonofabitch. Prospectin'? You got the fever, too?"

"Why not? Why should I get by on a lawman's wages while everybody else is getting rich?" The sheriff mounted his horse. "Wish the moon would come up. Hope these horses can see where they're going. I sure as hell can't."

Chapter Three

It was a sleepless, mind-torturing night for John McCrea. He lay on the ground between his blankets beside the Diamond J wagons. One half of a long bed tarp was under him and the other half was folded back over him. His pants and shirt were folded and used for a pillow. The sight of a dying man kept haunting him.

Maybe it was the sight of Old Levi drawing his last breath that brought back the memory. It was a memory that had haunted McCrea for over a year, one he could not ride away from no matter how far he went. It was his dad, lying on the ground beside the new house, what was left of it, like a scrap of paper crumpled and thrown away. Shot through the lungs. Dying. Trying to say something but unable to talk because of the blood burbling between his lips.

McCrea lay between his blankets and looked at the stars but saw only John McCrea Senior. He groaned aloud at the memory. And the anger. The terrible gut-wrenching anger that possessed him as he rode wildly into Roswell, carrying his old Colt .44-40 in its handmade holster.

Johnny McCrea the gunslinger. A very dangerous man. Killed three men in Roswell, New Mexico Territory. Johnny McCrea, the fastest gun in the West.

The frustration came back, too, the terrible mixture of anger and frustration that had him half crying when he had stomped into the Longhorn Saloon and found them there. He had found them drinking whiskey and playing cards as if nothing had happened. And then the chill. The chill that went through him, cooling him, cooling his mind, steadying his hand as he saw them grab for their guns.

Johnny McCrea, the cool, deadly gunman.

John McCrea groaned again and threw his arm over his eyes, trying to blot it out of his mind. Could he ever forget it? Would he ever be free of the memory? And the reputation?"

The Diamond J crew continued combing the high valleys and hillsides next day, bringing down a motley collection of cows, their calves and a few of the better bred Hereford bulls. By sundown they had about a hundred head gathered on a rocky meadow where the grass was stirrup high. They held them there until the cows and their calves found each other again, and went back to the wagons, their horses tired and footsore. Sheriff G.B. Harvey was waiting for them.

The crew jerked saddles off their horses, watched the horses roll on the ground and scratch their sweaty backs, then bowlegged it to the chuck wagon, planning to ease the growling in their stomachs.

"Better keep a horse up for him, Jud," the sheriff said and nodded toward McCrea. "I'm going to have to take him back to town with me."

"What for, Harv?" Olesky pulled his wool pants up higher and smoothed down his long moustache. "Whatta you got against him?"

McCrea came up beside Olesky. He said nothing but his face registered the same question.

"I've got several reasons, Jud." The sheriff spoke only to the Diamond J cow boss as if McCrea was another head of livestock to be talked about but not to. "First off, I don't know whether you know it or not but he's a professional gunslinger, a hoodlum. He killed three men down in the New Mexico Territory about a year ago."

"Huh?" Olesky turned to McCrea. "That so, John?"

"Well yeah, but—" McCrea shrugged. He had told the story before and no one had believed him.

Olesky squinted at McCrea. "You shot three men? Hell, I never even seen you raise yore voice to a man. And I never seen you with a gun." He turned to the sheriff. "Almost ever'body around here packs iron but John here. If he's a gunslinger he shore as hell ain't acted like it."

"He is, all right," Harvey insisted. "That's Johnny McCrea. I knew I'd heard that name before, but it took me awhile to remember where. He's the one, all right. Shot three men in a fight down at Roswell. Killed all three. Then lit out."

"Are you wanted by the law, John? Is that why you hired on here?"

"No," the sheriff answered for McCrea. "Not that I know of. Word is he claimed self-defense, and the law, what law they've got down there, let him go. No, I looked but I haven't seen any dodgers on him."

"Then why are you wantin' to take 'im to town?"

25

The rest of the Diamond J crew had gathered, looking at the sheriff and then looking at McCrea.

"Something's strange about his story. We looked over Old Levi's body, and he wasn't shot. When somebody around here wants to kill a man he shoots him. You say this man wasn't carrying a gun, and whoever killed that old sourdough apparently didn't have a gun, either."

Olesky pulled his pants up higher on his skinny hips. "Hell, Harv, is that any reason to arrest a man? 'Cause he doesn't pack iron? It was prob'ly that old feller's ticker."

The crew looked from McCrea to Olesky then to Harvey.

"That's not all. He said he was shot at, didn't he? Well, I looked and looked and the only empty shell casings I found were the ones that came from Old Levi's Henry. If someone shot at him there'd be some empty shell casings, wouldn't there?"

McCrea stood quietly, letting Olesky argue for him.

Olesky looked over the sheriff's head and squinted at the darkening sky, lost in thought. Finally, he said, "Yeah, you'd think so, but hell, whoever did the shootin' could have carried away his brass."

"I thought of that and it's possible. But you have to admit it's strange. Put that together with this man's reputation and what would you do if you was sheriff?"

"I dunno, Harv. I guess I'd want to keep 'im around where I could find 'im again, just in case. But I think I know John and I can't believe he's a hazard to anybody." The cow boss swallowed and his adam's apple dipped. "He's quiet and he never talks about hisself, but he's a good hand, and he shore never had any trouble with anybody on this outfit. Ain't that right, boys?"

A half-dozen cowboys nodded their heads in agreement.

"Well, it's like you said, Jud, I can't take a chance on having him quit the country."

"Where're you gonna keep 'im?"

G.B. Harvey studied the toe of his left boot. "Now that's a real problem. The courthouse and jail won't be finished for a few weeks, and until it is I've got no place to lock anybody up."

"Wa-al, I'd ask you to leave 'im here, shurff, but fact is he's drawin' his pay and leavin' in the mornin' anyway. Ain't that right, John?"

"Yeah," McCrea answered, "I've got a good reason. I don't usually quit an outfit before the job's done, but I've got a good reason."

"What's that, young fella?" the sheriff asked.

McCrea glanced around at the Diamond J crew. "I've never mentioned this, but I've got some land down in the Pecos Valley that I've been trying to sell. The Turkey Track outfit has made a good offer." He glanced at Olesky. "That's what the letter I got two days ago was all about. Trouble is, it took too long for that letter to catch up with me, and the Turkey Track wants to close the deal no later than October twenty-third. That's five days from tomorrow, isn't it? That's why I've got to be on my way."

"Uh-huh." The sheriff snorted. "You see, Jud, that's exactly why I have to take him into custody. He found a murdered man. His story don't hold water, and he's leaving the country. What would you do?"

"Aw, I still don't believe he's a killer." Judson Olesky pulled his pants up higher on his waist. "Hell, if he killed that old prospector, he would of just left the carcass there and said nothin'."

"Not necessarily. He's not dumb. Put it together, Jud. An old prospector is found dead—and he would have been found sooner or later, what with your crew riding those hills every day—and a cowboy with a bad reputation draws his pay and quits the country. What would you think?"

Olesky pushed his hat back and squinted at McCrea, then looked back at the sheriff. "What you're thinkin' then, shurff, is he just told us a story about findin' a dyin' man?"

"You figure it out."

"I can't believe it. And you said you got no place to lock a man up."

"No, but I want him where I can watch him. I can't lock him up, but I want him to see me every morning and every night. If he doesn't, I'll have flyers out on him, and I'll accuse him of murder. He won't get far."

Olesky looked toward the chuck wagon and saw the crew's horse wrangler scrape his supper plate and head for the rope corral that held the Diamond J remuda. He yelled at him. "Wait up, Joel. We might need a couple of hosses."

Joel waited, curious. Olesky touched McCrea on the shoulder.

"Far as I'm concerned, you're innocent 'til proved guilty like the law says, but I can't stand in the shurff's way."

"I understand." That was all McCrea had to say.

"You've got two hosses of your own in the remuda. Cut 'em out and I'll make out your time."

Nodding in agreement, McCrea didn't wait for supper but went to the corral, caught his two horses, loaded his bedroll and warbag on one and put his saddle on the other. He mounted, looked blankly at the sheriff, and followed when the sheriff got on his horse and headed toward Bluebird.

They rode in silence. G.B. Harvey tried to make conversation, to satisfy his curiosity if nothing else, but he got only the shortest possible answers from John McCrea.

"What happened down there in the Pecos Valley, young fella? I heard rustlers are making beef raising a dangerous occupation. You involved in that?"

"That was a year ago, sheriff, and no matter what I say, you won't believe me."

Harvey grunted. "I never met a gunslinger yet that didn't claim the other fella shot first. Is that what you're claiming?"

McCrea's mood was dark and getting darker. He had told the truth, but folks would rather believe the rumors. Twice now he had had to move on when the rumors caught up with him. And now, were it not for the fact that the county—what was the name of it? Justin County?—was a new county and had no jail yet, he would be locked up. "Dandy," he mumbled to himself.

"What was that?" The sheriff squinted at him in the near darkness. "Did you say something?"

"No."

"You're not very talkative, are you young fella?"

"Listen, sheriff." McCrea tried to reason with the lawman. "It's like I said back there at the wagons. It's important that I get back by the twenty-third. I might not get another offer for that land." His voice took on a bitter note. "It's just my luck, just my damn rotten luck that I happened to stumble over a dying man."

Chapter Four

Crystal Lee Brown had just locked the door when they rode up. She considered letting them in and setting some plates of leftovers before them. But then she recognized the sheriff and knew he had a home and a woman to cook for him, and the other man looked like a cowhand who would no doubt end up at The Palace sooner or later anyway. Wasn't that the man who rode into town in a hurry a day ago? Yes, he was the man with the pleasant face. But he seemed angry now. Something was bothering him. Oh well, he could find what he wanted at The Palace.

Crystal Lee and Maudie finished washing and stacking the dishes, mopped up and took off their aprons. "I'm goin' home and soak mah feet and I'm goin' right to bed," Maudie said. "Mornin' comes too early for this old darky."

"I'm sorry about this, Maudie. I certainly appreciate your help. I hired a man who appeared to be down on his luck to wash dishes, but he didn't show up. I'll try again in the morning to hire someone. Here." Crystal opened the cigar box which held the day's receipts and took out a gold eagle. "Maybe this will make you feel better."

The plump black woman smiled, showing strong healthy teeth. "It shore do, Miss Brown. There ain't nothin' like these old eagles to make a body feel better."

"You've earned it, Maudie."

They left through the back door, locking it behind them. Maudie went home to her Charlie, and Crystal went to her two-room cabin across the alley. She was bone weary, but she had to have a bath. She couldn't sleep well with a day's accumulation of perspiration sticking to her skin, and she had a longtime habit of bathing before going to bed.

She gathered an armload of firewood from a stack outside her cabin door and built a fire in a small cook stove. She pumped a bucket of water and put it on top of the stove to heat. Wearily, she closed the shutters on the windows, wondering if she would ever be able to get the broken one fixed. With all the building going on in Bluebird, it was hard to find someone handy with tools to work on such a small job. While the water warmed, she piled her reddish brown hair high on her head and pinned it there to keep it dry while she bathed. She tested the water with a finger, found it warm enough and lifted the bucket down onto a woven sisal mat. She undressed, dipped a washcloth in the bucket and began washing herself.

Crystal Lee Brown was a shapely young woman, but it was something she was not particularly proud of. She had been ogled too many times by men who had lust in their eyes, and she found that very uncomfortable. She wanted to be treated with respect for being a good human being, not for being shapely, but she knew that her background, when it caught up with her, made that difficult. When she bought clothes she chose garments that hid her figure. She hated to be ogled.

She had just toweled her ankles and had straightened up when her eyes caught a movement at the window, the one with the broken shutter. Someone was out there looking in at her. Quickly she grabbed her nightgown from a peg on the wall and wrapped it around her. Revulsion welled up in her followed by outrage. She blew out the lamp and sat on the bed in the dark. Angry thoughts crowded into her mind. If she were a man she would have a gun, and she would run out there and shoot somebody. That's what she would do if she were a man. Or would she?

She shook with anger. Someone had seen her naked. Someone had peeked in her window and watched her bathe. Whoever it was would probably tell about it and describe her to his cronies. Crystal clasped her hands together to stop them from shaking. She forced herself to calm down. The doors were latched from the inside. No one could get in. She was safe.

Slipping the nightgown over her head, she climbed into bed without relighting the lamp. She needed sleep, but in spite of her weariness, sleep wouldn't come. Would she never escape?

At one time a year ago, when she first came to Bluebird and bought the cafe, she thought she had escaped. Bluebird was a quiet little ranching town about eighty-five hundred feet high in the Sangre de Cristos. Surely she would not be recognized here, and for a time, she was happy. She worked hard, built up a good clientele and began thinking about her future. Now if only she could find a good man.

Then gold was discovered on nearby Willow Creek, and the riffraff began moving in. They came from all over the country, looking for wealth. Most were honest, hard-working prospectors, but as more and more gold was dug up and more and more of the prospectors got rich, more and more of the riffraff moved in, hoping to profit from the labors of others. Brawls were common. Even shootings. Poor old Sheriff Harvey, whose appointed job started out as a political plum, had more than he could handle.

The town was growing: the new saloon, the soon to be finished hotel, the courthouse. Men were sleeping in tents and tarpaper shacks, but new fine Victorian houses were going up, too. There was money to be made in Bluebird, and Crystal was sure she would soon find a buyer for her cafe. She would be leaving a profitable business behind, but she had to move on. Her past had caught up with her.

Crystal Lee Brown turned over on her stomach and put her face in the pillow. Was there no escape?

The streets were alive in Bluebird. Excitement was in the air. Gold. Men were getting rich. New veins were found almost every day. Why, just two days ago a man was digging a cellar for a new house and found gold. Deep holes were being dug all around the town, and mine head frames were going up over them. The Bluebird Mill was processing ore twenty-four hours a day, and another mill was being built just two miles east of town. Heavy freight wagons pulled by four-ups and six-ups rolled into town every day, and mining tools, building materials, and grub were bought up sometimes even before it was unloaded. And it wasn't only the prospectors who were getting rich. The freight line owners had jacked up their prices, and the merchants had jumped on the gravy train and vowed to get theirs. The one hotel in town doubled its rates and kept every room filled. A long, one-story log building, formerly used as a place to store wool, had been converted to a cot house, and the new owner was chuckling every night as he counted his receipts.

Men in jack boots, bib overalls, and wool caps were waiting outside the door to the Bluebird Cafe when Crystal Lee Brown and Maudie opened for business. They poured in, lined the counter, sat at the wooden tables with the clean checkered oil cloths and stared hungrily at the menu handwritten on a blackboard above the counter.

The first message on the slate was "Help Wanted. Good Wages."

Maudie groaned aloud when she saw the room fill up. "How in the world are we gonna feed 'em all, Miss Brown?"

"We'll just have to do the best we can, Maudie. I certainly wish someone would step up and ask for a job."

"You know what I wish, Miss Brown? I wish they'd hurry up and build that new saloon. I hear they're gonna feed people in there."

"The new hotel will have a dining room, too," Crystal said. "There seems to be plenty of business for everyone."

The two women each carried a coffeepot around the room and filled coffee cups. They had to apologize for the lack of cream. "I have a standing order for condensed milk with the wholesalers, Haley and Jones," Crystal told a miner, "but they're having the same problem I'm having. They can't keep up with the demand."

Almost everyone wanted bacon and eggs for breakfast with either hotcakes or biscuits. Crystal had not taken half their orders before she had to apologize again. "Haley and Jones promised a freight string would be coming in this afternoon, and they would bring more eggs."

"I'll give ya a buck apiece for two fried eggs." The words came from a man in dirty overalls and a Scotch cap on his head. "I ain't had no eggs since I left Arkansas, and I'll pay anything for 'em."

"That's certainly a fair price," Crystal answered. "But I'm afraid the few eggs I have left have already been ordered."

"Listen, little lady, I've got a rich vein, and I'll give ya a ounce of dust right now for a dozen of them hen fruits."

"I'll try to have some tomorrow, Mr. . . . ."

"Henessy, ma'am. Arkansas Henessy. Call me Arkansas. Ever'time somebody calls me mister I look behind me to see who they're atalkin' to."

Another voice joined the conversation, this one from the next table. "I'll make it five dollars per egg, miss, and I'll pay right now." The man who spoke wore a businessman's clothes and had a pleasant smile on his face. "I have the most promising discovery yet, and I can afford it. As a matter of fact," he said, leaning back in his chair and hooking his thumbs in the pockets of a flowery vest, "I noticed your For Sale sign, and I might be willing to talk business."

Crystal returned the smile. "I would be happy to talk with you about it, but later when I'm not so busy."

"I'll wait, miss."

Crystal went to the next table, taking orders. Soon they were out of biscuits, too, but they still had the makings for pancake batter, and they had a good supply of bacon left. Maudie was hurrying from the stove where she poured and flipped pancakes to the butcher block where she sliced meat. Crystal hurried as fast as she could, carrying platters of food, filling coffee cups, and all the while forcing herself to smile.

More than once she found silver coins on the tables, left by men who had struck a vein and could easily afford generous tips. And more than once she found that some of her customers had left without paying, men who had not struck it rich and were out of money. With the crowd and the clamor it was easy to leave without paying. But it evened out, Crystal reminded herself, and she didn't like to think of anyone's going hungry.

By seven o'clock the crowd had thinned out. Only a few men sat at the counter, and only two tables were occupied. Dirty dishes were everywhere. Crystal took a large tin pan from a hook on the wall and began filling it with dirty dishes. Another customer came in and sat at the counter, and Crystal saw that it was the cowboy she had last seen in the company of the sheriff.

"Good morning, sir," she said as she picked up the dirty dishes in front of him and placed them in the pan. "I'll take your order in a moment."

"That's all right, ma'am. Don't hurry on my account."

His pleasant southern drawl caused her to take a second look at him. He smiled briefly, and when he did, the corners of his grey eyes crinkled. He appeared to be a man who would rather smile than frown, but his smile slipped, and she could tell he had something to worry about.

"I must apologize," she said, "There isn't much left. But we can serve you some hotcakes and bacon."

"That'll be fine, ma'am. And take your time. I've got all day."

She tried to place the drawl. It wasn't quite Texas, but it was from somewhere in the Southwest. In spite of her forced smile, weariness almost overcame Crystal for a second, and the tired lines showed in her face as she wiped the counter in front of the cowboy.

"Pardon my saying so, ma'am, but you look like you could use some rest."

The forced smile was back as Crystal answered, "What I really need is some help."

"Can't you hire somebody?"

"No, apparently not. Seems there is no unemployment in Bluebird."

"That's sure too bad."

She fetched the coffeepot and poured him a cup of coffee, then resumed carrying dirty dishes. Soon, she placed a platter of pancakes and bacon in front of him. He thanked her and dug in, eating silently.

Crystal had just finished cleaning the last table when she was aware of someone standing beside her. She looked up. And up. The man was incredibly tall, at least six feet six inches. His light brown hair went with his light complexion and was parted in the middle. He had a thin blond moustache over a wide sensuous mouth. It was the man who had offered her five dollars apiece for eggs. "I'm Amos Tarr," he said. "I still would like to talk a little business with you."

Amos Tarr was expensively dressed with a cravat at his throat, the flowery vest, a finger-length black coat, and gray pants with a sharp crease down the front.

Crystal straightened up and wiped perspiration from her forehead with the back of her hand. "Perhaps later tonight, Mr. Tarr. I must get ready for the noon meal."

"Yes, of course. But will you tell me what you are asking for your enterprise here?"

She had already decided on a price and answered readily, "Two thousand dollars. That is for the building and all the equipment."

"Sounds reasonable to me, Miss Brown. I'll tell you what. Why don't we get together after you close tonight and see if we can arrange a sale."

Stepping back to where she could look up at Amos Tarr without straining her neck, Crystal answered, "All right. Where would you like to meet?"

"At the Palace. We can find a quiet corner to talk business."

She hesitated, trying to find the words to say what she wanted to say. Amos Tarr saw her hesitation. "Oh, how stupid of me. Of course you don't want to meet there. That's no place for a lady. I'm sorry I suggested it. Why don't you name the place?"

"Here," she said. "I'll have the Closed sign up, but if you will knock on the door I'll let you in."

Amos Tarr agreed and bowed. It was the first time in a year that Crystal had seen a man bow. He was every inch a gentleman, and she couldn't help being pleased.

When she walked past the cowboy at the counter she caught him staring at her and saw him look away quickly, embarrassed. She was not outraged or uncomfortable. His manner was not one of lust but of curiosity. She saw that his coffee cup was empty and hurried to refill it.

Chapter Five

The meal tasted delicious, and McCrea cleaned the last crumb from his plate before pushing it aside and concentrating on the remainder of the coffee. He tried not to show it, but he was curious about the girl who had waited on him. She was very pretty, with her reddish brown hair, large expressive brown eyes, and a mouth that smiled a lot. He liked the way she walked, back straight, shoulders squared. She had dignity. Class. It was the way her apron strings pinched in at the waist that revealed her trim figure. McCrea wondered why she wore a dress that seemed to be a size too large. But her face was drawn, and the smile was obviously forced.

Once she turned unexpectedly and caught him staring at her, and he was embarrassed. He wished he had the gift of gab that some men had so he could get acquainted.

Feeling someone standing behind him, McCrea turned on his stool and looked up. His superior height made McCrea uncomfortable.

"Pardon me," the tall man said, "but aren't you the cowpuncher who found the murdered prospector?"

"Yes, I am."

The tall man sat at the stool next to McCrea and turned toward him. "How did you happen to find him?"

"By accident. I was gathering cows and saw his camp." McCrea wished the man would leave. He didn't want to talk about what he had found.

"The way I heard it, he had been tortured. Is that right?"

McCrea shrugged and took a sip of the coffee. "Looked that way. The sheriff can tell you all about it."

The tall man was not put off. "The word going around is he was still alive when you found him. Did he say anything?"

"No."

"Are you sure? Seems like he would have said something." The man stared hard at McCrea. McCrea concentrated on his coffee cup. He didn't want to return the stare and didn't want to answer any more questions.

"He was dying. He couldn't talk."

"I see. Hmm. Very interesting. Well," the man said and stood up, towering over the cowboy, "I hope the sheriff finds out who did it. Terrible. Just terrible." He turned and left.

"Excuse me, sir." The young woman was facing McCrea on the other side of the counter. "Did I hear you say someone was killed?"

"Yes, ma'am."

"I overheard some conversation about that earlier, but I was too busy to pay attention. Do you mind if I ask if you know who it was?"

"The sheriff said his name was Levi, ma'am."

"Oh." She turned suddenly pale. "Levi? Oh my."

"Are you sick, ma'am? Do you need help?"

"No." She forced calmness into her voice. "It's just that—is the sheriff sure about the identity?"

"Said he knew him. Did you know him, ma'am?"

"Why yes, I—dead? I can't believe it. Murdered?"

"I'm sorry to be the one to tell you. Was he a friend?"

"Sort of. Yes, I guess so. I guess I knew him as well as anyone in town."

McCrea took another sip of coffee. "Does the sheriff know you knew him? You might be able to tell the sheriff something that would help him find out who did it."

"No, I—I didn't know him that well. He came in here often, and we served him. He didn't talk much, but he did tell me once he was wealthy and could buy me out if he wanted to."

"Did he like to brag?"

"No, I don't think so, but he seemed to want to impress us, to let us know he had means. He didn't have any friends. Someone told me he was suspected of murder."

"Was he wealthy? The sheriff said he made a strike somewhere."

"That's what I heard. He had plenty of money. In fact, he gave me some gold to keep for him. He said he didn't trust banks. I didn't want to keep it, but he insisted."

"Well, excuse my questions, ma'am. It's none of my business, but I'm curious. Why did he leave his money with you?"

"Apparently, he thought he could trust me. He obviously didn't trust very many people. And he didn't leave much. A handful of nuggets. I have no idea what they are worth."

"That's odd," the cowboy mused aloud, draining his coffee cup.

"Would you do something for me, Mr., uh, Mr. . . . ."

"John McCrea."

"Mr. McCrea. Would you tell the sheriff that I knew Mr. Levi? I don't think I know anything that would help in his investigation, but I'll help if I can."

"I'll tell him, Miss . . ."

"Brown. Crystal Lee Brown."

The cowboy stood up. "How much do I owe you?"

"Forty cents, please."

"That was mighty good chuck. It was the first woman-cooked meal I've had in a long while." He paid her with silver coins and left.

McCrea remembered that he was to report to Sheriff G. B. Harvey every morning, and he turned toward the sheriff's office, a converted one-room log cabin on Main Street. The plank sidewalk was crowded with pedestrians, and McCrea often found himself on a collision course with mining engineers in their green corduroys and lace-up boots, carpenters in their bib overalls, and miners in their heavy shoes and dirty wool pants held up with tight belts. Everyone seemed to be in a hurry, and McCrea was always the one to step aside to prevent a collision.

Heavy freight wagons rumbled down the street, some carrying ore from the mines and some carrying lumber from the saw mill. Teamsters yelled at their teams but used such words as "durn" and "dang" while they were in town. McCrea had to grin at one teamster who wanted so badly to swear that he was red in the face but didn't dare swear in public.

Sheriff G.B. Harvey was at his desk going through the latest wanted flyers that had come in the mail the night before. He looked up as McCrea entered, thumped the pile of flyers and said, "You aren't wanted anywhere that I can find."

McCrea's jaw muscles tightened. "Listen, sheriff." He was trying again to reason with the lawman. "Getting back to Roswell by the twenty-third is mighty important to me. I've told you everything I know about that killing, and you have no real reason to keep me here."

G.B. Harvey tilted his chair back on its hind legs and looked up at the cowboy. "You're staying here 'til I say you can go, and if you keep complaining I can still take you up to San Lomah and lock you up."

"Lordy," McCrea grumbled.

"What's that, young fella?"

"What are you doing, sheriff, to solve the puzzle?"

"I'm doing everything I can. I'm asking questions all over town. I've got to go up to San Lomah today, and I think I'll bring the coroner back with me. Maybe he can help."

McCrea told him about Crystal Lee Brown and her acquaintance with the murdered man, and the sheriff was interested. "Come to think of it, she probably knew him better than anyone else. Most folks around here figured he murdered his partner, and they wanted nothing to do with him, but she treated him nicely. I think Old Levi took a liking to her."

The sheriff thumped the flyers again. "Seems to me a man with your reputation ought to be wanted somewhere." He leaned back in his chair and squinted up at McCrea. "Way I heard it you killed three men in a fight down at Roswell in the New Mexico Territory. Is that right?"

McCrea only nodded.

"So you drifted up here, probably figuring to get rich in the gold fields but finding it easier to take somebody else's gold than to dig for your own."

Angry bitter words boiled out of McCrea. "That's plain stupid. If I was looking for easy money, why in hell was I out there working fourteen hours a day for a cow outfit?"

Sheriff G.B. Harvey jumped to his feet. "Don't yell at me, young fella. I can still slap handcuffs on you and take you up to San Lomah, and you'd better not forget it."

He was right and McCrea knew it. A lawman had the whole U.S. Army behind him, and he could insult others and get by with it. The cowboy backed up a step and forced himself to calm down.

"You said to report to you every morning, sheriff. That's why I'm here."

"Yeah, that's what I said. All right, go on, but don't go far. I want to see you here again about sundown."

It was boring, hanging around town with nothing to do. McCrea couldn't help thinking about getting his horses and heading south and to hell with the sheriff. If he timed it right, he could be back in the Territory before the sheriff knew he was gone. He was losing money by staying in Bluebird. The Turkey Track made it clear they had to have the deal closed by the twenty-third, and they had made the best offer he would get. It was a chance to sell out and start over somewhere.

With the money, he could head west to Arizona or maybe even to California where nobody had heard of Johnny McCrea. Yes, he could use the money he got from the Turkey Track and buy more land and a few cows and start over. Out there, he could shake off the memories that had tormented him for over a year, and he could be free.

And in the meantime, if he was lucky, Sheriff G.B. Harvey would find out who had killed Old Levi and would withdraw the warrant on him.

It was something to think about. But it wouldn't work. The sheriff would know exactly where he was headed. McCrea had already told him about the land deal in Roswell. And Roswell had a telegraph wire now. It wouldn't work.

If he cut and ran now, he would be a hunted man, and he still wouldn't be free. "Aw hell," he grumbled to himself.

He stood on the street awhile, then walked out of town a short way to look at the mining activity and to pass the time of day. He stopped and watched twenty or more men unload a heavy piece of machinery from a wide, flatbed wagon and hitch a four-mule team to it. He idly wondered where mankind would be without horses and mules, and anger surged up in him when he saw a mule skinner grab a bull whip and mercilessly beat the mules when they failed to drag the machine over the ground.

He knew he ought to keep his mouth shut, but he could not. The mules were lunging in their collars and were so disorganized that only one mule at a time was pulling. One of the lead mules went down on its knees with the effort, and the skinner whipped it first on the rump and then about the head. That did it.

"Hey," McCrea was running toward them. "Cut that out! Stop!"

The mule skinner turned to see who was yelling. McCrea reached him, yanked the whip out of his hand and threw it down. "I know it's none of my business but I just can't stand by and watch that."

The skinner, a wide-shouldered man with a floppy straw hat, a tobacco-stained beard, and a flattened nose, stared hard at McCrea a moment, then reached down and picked up the whip. "You're right, mister, it ain't none of your business." With a move so swift it caught McCrea by surprise, the skinner brought the whip up and struck McCrea across the face with the stock of it. The two men were too close together for the end of the whip to lash McCrea, but the blow from the stock hurt just the same. Instinctively, McCrea's right fist came up from hip level and smacked squarely into the middle of the skinner's beard. The skinner staggered back, cursing wildly.

Then a dozen pairs of hands grabbed McCrea, grabbed the skinner and held them apart. "None o' that, boys," a man's voice said, and McCrea saw a short, husky man in baggy overalls standing between him and the skinner. "I don't blame ya fer what ya done, mister, but we got work ta do here, and we ain't got no time fer fightin'."

McCrea struggled, but four or five men had hold of him, and he could not break free.

"I seen what happened, an' I don't blame ya," the man repeated, "but now ya got to go on about yer business and let us move this here machine."

McCrea hissed. "He wasn't about to move it that way. He's no teamster. He never gave his mules a chance."

"Y'er right, I'll allow ya that, an' he ain't aworkin' fer me no more. Now, if ya'll promise to do no more fightin', I'll order my men to turn ya loose."

McCrea met the man's gaze for a long moment, then said resignedly, "Well, it wasn't my business, and I guess I shouldn't have butted in."

"Turn 'im loose, boys. An' mister, if ya think you can get them mules to work with kindness, I'd like ta see ya do it."

"Hell, them mules'll kick him loose from his teeth if he tries sweet talkin' 'em," the bearded skinner put in. "And Mr. Henessy, you can just take your goddamn mules and go to hell. There's plenty of other jobs."

"Go to my shack, Wheeler, and tell 'em I said to give ya yer time." Henessy turned back to McCrea. "You wanta try, mister?"

The four mules had quieted down now, and the four lines were on the ground where the skinner had dropped them. McCrea picked up the lines, laced them into his fingers and pulled back on them to get the mules' heads up. The mules were watching him now, their long ears twitching. McCrea shouted, "All right, boys, hit up. Hit in there."

The lead team leaned into their collars, but the wheel team remained motionless. The skinner snickered. "Told you. There ain't but one language them animules understand."

Taking all four lines in his left hand, McCrea took the end of one line in his right hand and flicked it at the rump of the near wheel mule. "Hit it." The four mules went into their collars, but they were not pulling together. First the lead team pulled and slacked off, then the wheel team.

The skinner snickered again.

McCrea took the lines in both hands, pulled back enough to get the feel of the snaffle bits and each animal's mouth, then hollered, "Hit it. Get in there. Hit it."

The lead team lunged, but McCrea held them back until the wheel team was leaning into their collars, and hollered again, "Hit it." Then the four mules were pulling together. The machine moved a foot, another foot, and then the mules, powerful muscles straining, were pulling the machine over the ground, leaving deep furrows in the dirt behind it.

"Over here, over here," Henessy yelled, hurrying

ahead of the straining team. "Over here."

McCrea turned the mules toward a wide deep hole in the ground and guided them alongside it.

"Right here, right here."

It took less than a minute to get the machine up next to the hole, and Henessy was jumping with happiness. "Right here. That's it. Right here. Whoa, whoa."

"Ho-o-o," McCrea said, bringing the team to a stop.

"That's it, that's right on the spot. You can unhitch, mister."

After unhitching the team and driving them away a few yards, McCrea came back to stand beside Henessy. "What is that thing, anyway?"

"It's a steam engine. We're gonna use it to run a hoist. We ain't got the smokestack put on 'er yet, but we'll get 'er on. I got a lode down there that won't quit."

"A steam engine." McCrea walked around the machine, studying it. "I never saw one up close before. They say when you get one of these fired up, it'll outpull twenty mules."

Henessy poured tobacco from a Bull Durham sack into the corn cob bowl of a pipe, then offered the sack to McCrea. "It will fer a fact. This is the first 'un around here, but there'll be plenty more. Say." Henessy held out his right hand. "I'm Arkansas Henessy. I owe ya fer yer help. You ain't lookin' for a job, air ya?"

"No." McCrea rolled a smoke with a paper he took from his shirt pocket and Henessy's Bull Durham. "I never worked around machinery, and I don't think I'd like it."

"Y'er a cowhand, ain't ya? Ain't that a purty good life?"

"It is if you own the cows." McCrea grinned. "But if

you work for somebody else it's, uh, well I guess it's better than most kinds of work. It's all I've ever done."

"You here to do a little prospectin', maybe?"

"No. I'm here because, uh—"

"Say," Henessy cut in, "I'll bet I know who ya air. Y'er that cowhand that found Old Levi, ain't ya?"

"Yep."

"Say, is it true what I heerd—that somebody burned his feet atryin' to make 'im tell where his strike is?"

"It looked that way." McCrea wanted to move on now, but he didn't want to be rude. "I've, uh, got to see to my horses."

"Let me pay ya for what ya done." Henessy dug into his baggy overalls and pulled out a worn cowhide wallet fat with paper money.

"No, I didn't do anything. It didn't take more than two minutes. I can't take money for that."

"Well hell." Henessy stuck out his right hand again. "If ya ever need a job or anything, holler."

"I'll do it." McCrea grinned.

Chapter Six

By late afternoon McCrea was thinking that maybe he should have taken the job Henessy offered. It would have enabled him to report to the sheriff regularly, and it would have given him something to do. Without a job he was bored. He waited until after the shift changed at the mines and the men without families had been fed, then went back to the Bluebird Cafe. The pretty young woman with the dark red hair was still there. Of course she was, McCrea thought, she owns the place. Or, he wondered as he took a seat at the counter, was her hair reddish brown? Anyway, it was thick and curly and hung to her shoulders. She was very pretty.

And she was very tired. McCrea could see the fatigue in the lines of her face as she hurried from customer to customer, serving them, forcing herself to smile. As tired as she was, she carried herself erect, with dignity. He admired her and wondered about her. How did she happen to be here in a small mountain town? Did she have a family? What kind of people are her family? Is she a widow? How did she happen to own a cafe? He watched her approach and matched her smile. Her smile widened.

"Good evening, Mr. McCrea. Can I interest you in some roast beef with boiled potatoes and carrots?"

"That sounds fine."

She had to pause for a second while she wiped a strand of hair from her eyes, and again her smile slipped for a second. "Coming right up, sir."

By the time McCrea finished his meal, the place was nearly deserted and, as before, dirty dishes were everywhere. Maudie came out of the kitchen to help pick them up. "Miss Brown, why don't you set a spell," Maudie pleaded, sympathy in her eyes. "I can clean up in here."

"No, Maudie. If you can stand it so can I."

"I swear, Miss Brown, if you don't rest a minute, your laigs are gonna fold up under you."

"With both of us working, it won't take long."

McCrea finished his coffee and sat there a long moment. He looked up as Crystal Lee Brown gathered his dirty dishes and spoke thoughtfully. "Suppose—suppose I don't have any money and can't pay for my meal. What would you do?"

She stopped what she was doing and studied his face, trying to determine whether he was serious. "Well, Mr. McCrea, I can't run a business serving customers who don't pay, but if you really don't have any money, I, uh—"

"Suppose I offer to work it out? I've washed dishes since I was knee-high to a coyote."

"We certainly could use some help, and if you want to work I'll pay you good wages, but you don't look like a man who would have to wash dishes for a living."

"Not for a living," McCrea said, "but for an evening.

53

I'll work this evening and maybe tomorrow you can find some permanent help. How's that?"

"That would be fine, Mr. McCrea, if you are sure you want to. You don't have to. You can pay me later."

McCrea stood up and began rolling up his sleeves. He grinned. "Just show me to them."

Conversation was light as the cowboy worked over the tub of warm sudsy water. At one time, Maudie tried to tie an apron around his waist, but he declined it. "I don't mind doing a woman's work once in a while," he said pleasantly, "but I'll be darned if I'm going to dress like one."

Maudie chuckled, and when Miss Brown came in from the dining room, she repeated what McCrea had said. Miss Brown chuckled too. "I don't think you have to worry about looking feminine, Mr. McCrea."

With the three of them working, it took about two hours to get the place cleaned up and everything put away. Crystal Lee Brown invited the cowboy to sit at the work table with her and Maudie and finish the coffee.

"You are really efficient, Mr. McCrea. Where did you learn to wash dishes?"

"At home. My dad and I batched it on a little cow outfit. My mother was a good housekeeper, and my dad always said there was nothing more depressing than a dirty house, and after my mother died he saw to it that I kept it clean."

"Do you cook too?"

"When I have to." McCrea nodded toward a pot of red beans simmering on the stove. "That sure smells good. It smells like home. My dad always said beans were his favorite fruit."

"They seem to be very popular around here, but

cooking them at this altitude takes all day." Miss Brown smiled. "I've learned to keep beans in three pots, one pot soaking, another cooking, and another ready to serve."

They were silent, sipping their coffee, then she asked, "Where is home, Mr. McCrea, if you don't mind my asking?" And then she wished she had not asked. The cowboy's smile faded quickly and a worried look came into his grey eyes. It was a worried and perhaps even a haunted expression. The cowboy was troubled. Crystal Lee Brown could sympathize with him. Whenever anyone asked about her background, she felt the same way.

She tried to find the words to apologize, but her thoughts were interrupted by a loud knocking on the front door.

"Oh, I almost forgot. That must be Mr. Tarr." She went to the door and allowed Amos Tarr to enter. The tall man took off his beaver hat.

"I must apologize for being late, Miss Brown, but I had other business to take care of. I'm pleased to find you're still here."

She invited him to sit at the table with McCrea and Maudie. His expression showed surprise at seeing the cowboy there, but he immediately smiled to conceal his surprise. "Nice to see you again, Mr. McCrea, isn't it?"

"John McCrea. It's my pleasure." McCrea stood up and rolled down his sleeves. "I'll be going now, Miss Brown."

"Stay awhile, Mr. McCrea. Make yourself a sandwich out of the remainder of the roast. You must be hungry again after all that work."

McCrea paused. "Well, it would be a shame to let it spoil, and I could stand another bite. Can I fix a sandwich for anyone else?"

"Not me," said Maudie. "I'm too fat already and I got to go home to my Charlie. I already fixed him a couple of samwiches."

"I'll pass too." Miss Brown smiled.

"Mr. Tarr?"

"No thank you. It was nice of you to ask. Now then." He turned his attention to Miss Brown. "You said two thousand dollars, right?"

"That's right, Mr. Tarr."

"I accept. I'll give you my note, and as soon as the bank here opens for business you can convert it to cash. How's that?"

"Why, that would be agreeable, but the bank has not been completed yet, and I understand it won't open for another week or two."

Amos Tarr took a thin black cigar from a vest pocket and lit it. "You understand my position, Miss Brown. I don't carry that kind of cash, and my bank account is in St. Louis. When the new bank opens, I will transfer my account, but in the meantime I'm writing drafts on the bank in St. Louis, or writing notes."

Miss Brown was silent a moment, thinking. Amos Tarr went on. "I don't blame you for not trusting a stranger. If you need cash right away, I can spare a hundred or two, but if you don't, why don't you take my paper and just wait until the new bank opens. We can draw up a contract in such a way that if for any reason you do not receive the agreed upon amount in cash within, oh, say one month, the enterprise reverts back to you."

Nodding in agreement, Miss Brown answered, "That sounds reasonable. But there is no lawyer in Bluebird to draw up such a contract."

"But there is a notary public. The sheriff, G.B. Harvey, himself has notary powers. He will attest to it. And, Miss Brown, you are an intelligent woman and I daresay a literary one. You can draw up the contract yourself if you want to."

Amos Tarr leaned back in his chair and took a deep drag from his cigar. He blew smoke toward the ceiling, careful not to allow it to drift toward Miss Brown or McCrea. "I wish things were more up to date here, Miss Brown, and we could do business the way we do it in St. Louis, but in this primitive land one must improvise." He smiled pleasantly at McCrea. "How does this sound to you, Mr. McCrea?"

"I'm no lawyer either," McCrea answered, "but I have been in a few cattle and land deals. If the contract is written in a simple language, Miss Brown, you either get your money or you keep your cafe."

Amos Tarr blew more smoke toward the ceiling and beamed. "You see, folks, I am investing heavily in the town of Bluebird. This town is booming and it is going to continue to boom. I'm lucky enough to have gotten my hands on a very rich gold mine just east of town, and I am getting in on the ground floor. I bought up good building lots when the price was low and sold most of them already at a handsome profit. I am building a new hotel and nightspot. My new club, when it is finished, will offer everything a club in St. Louis offers, including gambling and, uh—" Here Amos Tarr realized he had started to say something that would not be proper, and he cleared his throat hastily.

McCrea couldn't help noticing that Crystal Lee Brown's face had turned pale, and he wondered how she could be embarrassed that easily.

"I'm organizing a mining company," Amos Tarr went on, "and capitalizing it at one hundred thousand shares of common stock at ten dollars per share." He blew more smoke toward the ceiling and smiled affably, his thin blond moustache widening with the smile. "They will snap it up. You see, folks, the most the money lenders can get in the East is about seven percent per annum. That is tops. Here in the gold fields they can get two percent per month. Easily. They are looking for investment opportunities here."

"Well, pardon my asking, Mr. Tarr," McCrea said carefully, "and I know it's none of my business, but I can't help wondering why you want the Bluebird Cafe."

"You're no ordinary cowhand are you? Well, I'll put it this way. A cafe would be a source of immediate cash income. You are selling your product and your services too cheap, Miss Brown. I will add another cook, another waitress or two, some kitchen help, and I'll double, even triple, your prices and still have all the business they can possibly handle." He leaned back in his chair, pleased with himself. "I'll be taking in money as fast as I can count it."

Everyone was silent for a long moment. McCrea finished his sandwich. Crystal Lee Brown looked down at her hands folded on top of the table. Finally, Amos Tarr spoke again. "I hope I haven't talked you into not selling."

"Oh, no. When do you want to take over?"

"As soon as I can hire some help. I'll send up to Denver. I can get all the help I want there. I would appreciate it, Miss Brown, if you would continue managing the place a few more days until my new staff arrives. The receipts will be yours, of course, until I formally take over. And I'll see that you get some help immediately. I take it, Mr. McCrea, that you are not permanently employed here."

"No, just helping out."

Standing, towering over everyone, Amos Tarr offered his right hand to Miss Brown. "Then we have a deal?"

She stood and took his hand. "Yes. I'll get right to work on the contract. Meanwhile, we will open for business as usual in the morning."

"I'll send someone to help with the work. You can count on it." Amos Tarr turned to leave, then looked back at McCrea. "I'll be happy to buy you a drink, Mr. McCrea. Unless you are planning to stay longer."

"No." McCrea stood up. "It's time for me to leave. Sure, I'll have a drink with you."

The Palace Saloon was so crowded there wasn't even standing room at the bar, but men stepped back when they saw Amos Tarr coming. It wasn't just his size, it was also his air of importance: his aura of money and power. And Amos Tarr was a gentleman. He was polite and courteous to everyone, and men, even tough men, appreciated that.

"What's your pleasure?" he asked McCrea as they stood at the mahogany bar. The long hand-carved bar occupied one side of the room, and wooden tables and chairs filled the other side.

"Whiskey and water."

The bartender ignored other customers long enough to serve McCrea his whiskey and Amos Tarr his brandy. The cowboy tossed his drink down in a gulp and sipped the water. The tall gentleman sipped his brandy and rolled it around in his mouth before swallowing it.

"I don't mean to be critical," he said with a smile, "but

you miss the pleasure of drinking good liquor. Good liquor is intended to be savored, not, if you'll pardon the expression, gulped."

"You're probably right," McCrea said conversationally, "but I guess I've drank too much whiskey that couldn't be called good liquor."

The six-foot-six Amos Tarr threw his head back and laughed a hearty laugh. "I know what you mean. I've gotten hold of some of your frontier whiskey a time or two myself."

"Well, as the fellow says," McCrea replied and signaled the bartender for a refill, "booze is booze, and it's the kick that most men want anyhow, not the taste."

Amos Tarr laughed again and insisted that McCrea try some of his brandy. "I had to order a case of it from Denver, and I keep it here for my personal pleasure."

McCrea accepted the brandy, but he was not ready to agree to everything Amos Tarr said. He tasted it and put it down.

"Well? Good, isn't it?"

"It is if you're hungry. But I'd rather have whiskey than fruit juice." He smiled to show he was joking.

The tall man laughed again. It was easy to make Amos Tarr laugh.

The two men drank and made small talk about the cattle business, cattle prices, and huge land transactions they both had heard about.

"I became aware," Amos Tarr said after taking another sip of his brandy, "that you know something about business. If you don't mind my asking, where are you from originally?"

As before, when that question came up, McCrea suddenly became morose. He shrugged his shoulders as a hint that he did not want to answer. But Amos Tarr's curiosity, for a moment, got the better of his good manners.

"I've been trying to remember where I heard your name, and I think I've got it now. Weren't you in some sort of shooting scrap down south somewhere?"

McCrea only grunted and shrugged again. He was suddenly uncomfortable.

"As I recall," Amos Tarr went on, "you were described by some as being one of the fastest guns in the West."

The cowboy downed his whiskey and prepared to leave. "Thanks for the drink, Mr. Tarr. I've about had my fill for tonight."

"Don't leave," Amos Tarr said. "Forgive my curiosity. I won't mention it again."

McCrea paused, and the tall man continued, "It's none of my business." He signalled the bartender for a refill. "Speaking of guns, I've got one I'd like to show you. It's a Peter Paul Mauser, seven millimeter, with a bolt action. I had the stock custom-made and engraved to match the engraving on the plate."

McCrea pondered the offer. It was too early to turn in for the night, and there was nothing else to do. "All right, but I'm paying for this one."

The drinks were delivered and McCrea tossed his down. "Yeah, I've seen one of those, I think. At least the one I saw had a bolt action. It was a good gun, but it wouldn't do to carry on a saddle. Can you hit anything with it?"

"I must admit I haven't had many opportunities to fire it. I came out here to hunt elk with it, and it was while I was here that I realized the potential for investment."

That got the conversation around to the gold fields and

mining prospects in the Bluebird area. "I've been an investor all my life," the tall, well-dressed man said, "and I can't pass up an opportunity." He chuckled. "An old prospector named, uh, Smith, saw me in here one night and offered to sell me his valuable gold mine.

"Well." Amos Tarr took another sip, rolled it around in his mouth and swallowed. "I wasn't the eastern dude he thought I was, but I was interested. But instead of immediately laying out the cash, I hunted up one of the mining engineers and had him take some samples. And wouldn't you know it," Amos Tarr said and chuckled again, "the old-timer was right. Only he didn't realize it."

Still chuckling, he went on. "Smith thought he was selling me a worthless mine. He thought the vein had petered out. I found out he had only scratched the surface, and when he offered it to me for two hundred dollars, I bought it for one hundred and fifty.

"Now." Amos Tarr smacked his lips with pleasure. "I have one of the most—if not the most—valuable mines in Colorado, and I have the nuggets to prove it. Why, the first load of ore we took out assayed at two thousand dollars per ton. And look at this." He took a thumb-sized nugget from a pocket inside his coat. "This little rock alone is worth about three hundred and fifty dollars."

McCrea downed his whiskey, let it burn its way down his throat and into his stomach, and took a sip of water to stop the burning. "Well, I guess that's one explanation why some men are rich and some are poor."

"You're right. Some men seize upon an opportunity and others pass it by."

"Of course," McCrea added, "it helps to have the money to take advantage of an opportunity when it comes along."

The tall man threw his head back and laughed again. "You're absolutely correct, Mr. McCrea."

McCrea grinned but said no more for a time. When Amos Tarr's laughter subsided, the tall man turned serious. "Listen, Mr. McCrea—may I call you John?—listen, speaking of opportunities, I can't help being intrigued by that other old prospector, that Mr. Levi. I've done some checking, just out of curiosity, and I've learned that he never filed a claim on anything, yet he obviously had struck a rich vein somewhere. Wherever it is, it's just laying there waiting for someone to find it and file on it."

The cowboy only grunted.

"When word of his death got around, the first question everybody asked was whether he gave any hint of its whereabouts."

McCrea knew what was coming, and he wished he were somewhere else. Now that the question had come up again, he was wondering if maybe that wasn't the reason Amos Tarr was being so friendly in the first place. He cleared his throat and spoke slowly and thoughtfully. "It's just like I told the sheriff, Mr. Tarr—"

"Call me Amos, won't you?"

"Amos, the old man was still alive when I found him, but just barely. He tried to talk but couldn't get the words out. He died within two minutes after I found him. I don't know where the mine is."

"I see." Amos Tarr was silent. McCrea thought he saw disappointment in the tall man's face. Well, that was too bad.

Suddenly, McCrea was shoved roughly up against the

bar, causing him to spill the shot glass of whiskey he was holding. He spun around, puzzled.

An angry voice boomed, "You're the sonofabitch that done it." It was the bearded, flat-nosed mule skinner who was fired earlier that day by Arkansas Henessy. "You're the sonofabitch that got me fired."

Chapter Seven

The broad-shouldered mule skinner shifted into a boxer's stance, feet apart, left foot ahead of the other, doubled fists held chin high with the left fist out in front and chin tucked in. "I'm gonna learn you to mind your own goddamn business." He jabbed with the left fist, and it connected with McCrea's chin.

Men stood back, giving them room. Amos Tarr stepped back but said, "Watch him. He's a bully."

The left fist shot out again, and McCrea felt the shock run through his head, leaving his vision a little blurred.

He couldn't just stand there and let the skinner beat him to pieces. He knew he had to get his guard up and hit back. He tried a roundhouse swing. The skinner bobbed and weaved expertly, grinning. Someone warned, "Keep away from 'im, cowboy. He's a prizefighter."

Again the left jab, and again McCrea's head was snapped back. He tried to remember what he had been advised to do when he was a kid getting into school-yard brawls. Keep your dukes up. Move around. Hit straight out with your left fist and keep the right ready. He turned so that his back was no longer against the bar and backpedaled. He tripped over a spittoon and almost fell. Before he could regain his balance, the skinner was on him, punching, jabbing, pounding.

McCrea covered his face and head with his arms, elbows forward, and blinked, trying to clear his vision. He saw the skinner grin cruelly.

"You cowpunchers can't whip the shit off your shirttail. I'm gonna beat you 'til you holler for Mama." He jabbed again.

McCrea's left arm was across his face for protection. Now he whipped it back, fist doubled. The skinner, believing he had the cowboy beaten, had let his guard down for a second. McCrea's fist caught the end of his nose, and the skinner staggered back in pain. But that just made him angrier.

The broad-shouldered man bored in then, fists swinging, pummeling. McCrea ducked under the onslaught and the two men collided. Then McCrea found himself in a bear hug. Like two lovers in an embrace, the two men grunted and strained. The skinner had his arms around McCrea's rib cage, squeezing. He was powerful. Breath whooshed out of McCrea. His ribs ached.

McCrea tried pounding him in the face, but the skinner buried his face in McCrea's shoulder and squatted. They fell back against the bar, and the cowboy felt his knees going weak.

It was then that McCrea discovered another use for his high-heeled riding boots, the boots with the hard leather shanks made for comfort in a stirrup. He planted the shank of his right boot just below the skinner's left knee and brought it down the shin hard, peeling the skin.

Grunting with pain, the skinner loosened his hold and

stepped back, favoring his left leg. McCrea hit him in the face with a left, followed with a right roundhouse swing, then another left. The skinner staggered back but regained his balance and went into his boxer's stance again. He was still full of fight, but now he was not grinning.

Men were shouting. Some were offering encouragement to the skinner, others to the cowboy. They had formed a circle around the combatants. They were enjoying the fight.

Another left jab caught McCrea on the jaw. He sidestepped to his right, away from the skinner's left fist. The next left jab whistled past McCrea's ear, and at the same time McCrea's right fist shot straight out. It connected. But the skinner's heavy beard provided some protection from the shock, and he was not hurt. The two men glared at each other, the skinner in his boxer's stance, McCrea ready to dodge the left jab.

Men shouted. Bets were offered, accepted. Money was laid on the bar.

The skinner was breathing heavily, and it became evident that McCrea was in better condition. Someone offered three to two on the cowboy. Someone else yelled, "Come on, fight. Don't just make faces at each other."

McCrea tried another right-hand punch. The skinner bobbed and weaved, and it missed. Then, before McCrea could draw his fist back, the skinner's left jab caught him again, and that was followed by a powerful right cross. McCrea fell back against the bar, his ears ringing. He got his hands up before his face to ward off more blows.

The betting odds shifted to favor the skinner.

Feeling victory again, the skinner bored in. He had the cowboy backed against the bar now. He couldn't get away. After all, he had fought in the ring, and the cowboy knew nothing about boxing. From here on it was going to be a pleasure. With a cruel snicker, he threw punch after punch. Most of them landed on the cowboy's arms, but some found their target. When the cowboy tried to duck under the punches, the skinner just cooly stepped back and took aim. He hit the cowboy on the ear, on the forehead, on the side of the head, and he knew the cowboy was hurt.

But why didn't he go down?

Someone loudly offered five to one on the mule skinner.

McCrea had been knocked around by livestock all his life. He had been kicked, butted, knocked down, stomped on, dragged. He had been thrown off horses so hard he didn't think he would ever be able to stand again, but he had had to get up, get back on the horse and take his punishment. "That's cowboyin'," his dad had said. "If you can't take it, Johnny, you'd better move to town." McCrea had taken it.

But now he was taking the worst beating of his life, and it seemed there was nothing he could do to prevent it. It never occurred to him to give up. He just had to take it. He felt the blow hammer the side of his head, and again his knees went weak. He was going down whether he wanted to or not. He had to stay up, had to fight back. The yelling of the men around him reminded him of the yelling of the boys in the school yard. "Hit him. Hit him back, Johnny."

McCrea uncovered his head and started swinging. His punches were wild but so furious that the skinner did not backpedal fast enough.

"Hit him back, Johnny."

With desperation, McCrea threw punch after punch, felt two of them connect. He swung again and again but missed. Then something in his mind told him that he was wasting energyy. The winners in a fight were the men who stayed calm, took aim. Stay calm, McCrea, his mind told him.

The skinner was worried now. He wished he had not drunk so much since he had quit prizefighting. He was winded. His arms were becoming heavy. Two of the cowboy's blows had hurt. The cowboy was tougher than he had expected. He was hitting back. The skinner had to finish him off, and he had to do it right now.

He waded in. But now he was swinging wildly. His training as a boxer was forgotten. He had to smash that cowboy. He forgot his boxer's stance and waded in.

McCrea sidestepped, circling away from the left jab and making the skinner reach far out for him with the right fist. A right cross grazed McCrea's chin, doing no harm, and then McCrea's own right fist came around in a looping swing from the shoulder and connected with the skinner's jaw. The skinner staggered back, blinking in disbelief. He should have won this fight by now. The cowboy should be down, begging for mercy.

A weak jab caught McCrea in the mouth, but the cowboy was beyond caring. All he wanted now was to hit. Hit and hit. He cooly watched for an opening, shot his right fist out and felt it connect with the skinner's nose. The skinner brought his hands up to ward off more blows to the face. McCrea stepped closer and drove his left fist into the skinner's middle. The skinner's guard dropped. Another hard right hand blow caught the skinner in the mouth. He tried to backpedal, but McCrea stayed on him, shooting jabs, connecting.

The skinner was beaten. His breath was whistling in his lungs. His arms were so heavy he could barely raise them. He wished a bell would ring, ending the round. He wanted to run. He turned his back to McCrea and staggered forward.

But McCrea had taken a beating in a fight he did not start, and he wanted to return the punishment. He caught the skinner by the right shoulder, spun him around and delivered a right-hand punch that came up from his knees. The blow caught the skinner squarely in the mouth and sent him sprawling. He stayed down, unable to move.

Cheers went up from the crowd, and men who had bet on the cowboy began collecting their money. McCrea turned to the bar and leaned on it for support. He, too, was breathing heavily, and his arms also were tired. Men slapped him on the back. Amos Tarr moved up beside him.

"That was a good fight, Johnny. A very good fight. You just whipped a man who was very hard to whip."

McCrea only grunted.

"You're the kind of man I'd like to call a friend."

McCrea's breathing was returning to normal.

"I'd consider it an honor to buy you another drink as soon as you feel like it."

"In a minute."

Then a shout came from behind McCrea, a warning. "Look out, he's got a gun." McCrea spun. The skinner was sitting up. He had a small Remington double-barreled derringer in his hand. He pointed it at McCrea.

There was no escape. No matter how fast McCrea moved it wouldn't be fast enough. The skinner's lips curled in a sneer. His finger tightened on the trigger.

A shot came from beside McCrea, and the top of the skinner's head blew off and splattered against an overturned table behind him. He pitched back. His pistol barked once but the shot hit the ceiling. McCrea spun again and saw Amos Tarr holding an easy to conceal gun, a Colt .41 caliber "house pistol."

The tall man spoke calmly. "I never go unarmed on the frontier." He smiled at McCrea. "I couldn't help you when the fight was fair, but that wasn't fair."

John McCrea had spent one night in the wool house turned cot house, and one night was enough. The coughing, hacking, and spitting from the fifty or more men had kept him awake most of the night. He went to Johnson's Corrals, picked up his bedroll, threw it over his shoulder and walked out away from the town buildings and roads. He untied his bed and rolled it out in the grass at the bottom of a hill, pulled off his boots and pants and crawled between the blankets.

When daylight awakened him, he rolled up the bed and carried it back to Johnson's. There, he washed his face in a stock tank and wished he had a place to shave. But after feeling his face, he decided it was too sore to shave anyway. He went to The Palace just to look at himself in the bar mirror.

"Lordy," he mumbled. One eye had a dark quarter circle over it, his upper lip was swollen, and he had a small knot on the side of his head, just under his hat.

Only a few men stood at the bar, and the bartender had time on his hands. He moved casually over to McCrea. "The sheriff give you any trouble?"

"No." McCrea grinned crookedly. "He wanted to. He

was just looking for a chance to give somebody some trouble."

"It was that dandy, that Amos Tarr, that talked him out of it."

"Yeah, it seems the sheriff listens when big money talks."

"Never seen a lawman that didn't. But hell, he had to. There had to be fifty witnesses that saw what happened."

"Guess my luck ain't all bad." McCrea grinned again and felt a pain in his upper lip.

"What're you drinking?"

"Coffee. That's all I want. I drank enough booze last night to last me awhile."

The bartender nodded toward a connecting room. "You have to get it in there. But I wouldn't eat any of their flapjacks. They taste like cow shit." He went to draw a beer for a thirsty miner.

McCrea's next thought was to slip in among the other customers at the Bluebird Cafe and hope the pretty woman, Crystal Lee Brown, wouldn't notice him and his beat-up face. But when he looked in he saw the place was crowded with men standing, waiting for someone to leave so they could sit and be served.

"Lordy," McCrea murmured. He walked to the sheriff's office, boot heels thumping on the boardwalk. The sheriff wasn't in yet. McCrea stood outside the office twenty minutes until G.B. Harvey came along, then followed him inside.

"Have you learned anything, sheriff? I might still be able to make it to Roswell in time."

"Well, we learned what killed Old Levi. It wasn't a bullet. It was his heart."

"What? His heart?"

"Yep. Old Doc Handley cut him open and the blood that came out was thick as molasses. The doc said that's a sign of a bad heart. We figure the pain and everything he went through was just too much for him."

"All right, now you know he could have been tortured by anybody with or without a gun. That ought to take some of the suspicion off of me."

"No it don't. I'll tell you something that's easy to think. It's easy to think nobody from here followed him and somebody just happened onto his camp, figured he had something on him worth stealing and done him in."

McCrea stared hard at the sheriff. "So you still think I did it. You think I killed him for whatever I might find on him."

"It does look suspicious. And you're a troublemaker. No doubt about that."

Holding the sheriff's gaze, McCrea said, "I never saw him before. I didn't know him from Adam's off ox."

G.B. Harvey finally looked away. "You might be telling the truth about that. Might be. I don't know yet." He glanced back at the cowboy. "That's the reason you're still walking around free."

McCrea couldn't resist being sarcastic. "Oh, ain't I the lucky one, though." His upper lip hurt when he tried to sneer.

Chapter Eight

The breakfast crowd had thinned out now, and Crystal Lee Brown expected to see the cowboy with the southern drawl come in. When he did not, she couldn't help wondering why. She had heard about the fight and the shooting, and she was worried that he might be injured. Did he hire out on one of the cattle ranches in Justin County? Would she ever see him again? Now that she had more help, she could slow down a little and do more thinking, but that wasn't necessarily good. Did she imagine that some of her customers that morning were looking at her with a lusty interest? Had the message gotten around? Silently, she hoped the bank would be finished and open for business ahead of schedule so she could get her money from Amos Tarr and be on her way.

On her way where? Where could she go that her background wouldn't catch up with her?

Amos Tarr came in and folded his tall frame into a chair at one of the vacant tables. She hurried to him and asked for details about the shooting the night before. He told her about it in detail and said he felt terrible about having to shoot a man, but he couldn't just stand by and watch an innocent man murdered.

"Was Mr. McCrea hurt?" she asked.

"Oh no. He received some bruises, but he's not hurt."

That satisfied her curiosity, and she took his order for breakfast. When she brought it to him, she thanked him for sending a man to help and showed him one of the nuggets that Old Levi had left with her.

"Do you think it's worth anything?" she asked.

Amos Tarr took it, examined it and answered, "At least three hundred dollars. Did he leave anything else with you?"

"No, just three of these. He had more. I'll turn them over to the sheriff."

"Why don't you keep them? You earned them, and I doubt if he has any next of kin."

"I'll ask Mr. Harvey what to do with them."

"Suit yourself. The old man was pretty friendly with you, wasn't he?"

"Oh, he didn't talk much, but he did seem to like the food."

"Did he ever say anything about the location of his mine? He never filed a claim, and whoever finds it will probably be rich."

"No. He talked, uh, kind of senseless sometimes, and I seldom knew what he was talking about."

"You ought to give it some thought, Miss Brown. I'll make a deal with you. If you happen to remember something, tell me and we'll split the profits."

"I'll think about it, but he never talked much about his mine, not even in a senseless way."

"You think about it, Miss Brown. I know you don't want to go tramping around up there, and if you can supply me with a clue and I find it, I'll see you get fifty percent."

When she didn't answer, he went on. "Try to remember everything he said. There just might be a clue in some of his prattle."

She picked up dirty dishes from the next table and answered, "I'll think about it."

The bartender was right about the pancakes at The Palace. John McCrea had never tasted worse cooking, but he managed to wash a few of them down with strong black coffee. He paid and went back out on the street.

A cool wind was blowing in from the west, and the aspen trees up on the hillsides were rapidly shedding their leaves. Their golden color mixed with the greens of the pine, and spruce made the hills spotted. Winter was not far ahead, and McCrea knew that winter in the high country was severe and lengthy. A southerner all his life, he had no wish to stay there. Good country in the summer, sure, with good green grass in every park and meadow. But, as Judson Olesky had said, the growing season only lasted three or four months, and once the grass was cropped off there was no more until the next spring.

McCrea had heard that the U.S. Government was considering setting aside huge hunks of land in the mountains as public domain and would soon stop offering it for sale. Talk was that stockmen could still graze on it, but they would have to pay a grazing fee. The days of the free range would soon be over. He knew it and everybody knew it, and that was why the Turkey Track was willing to pay a good price for his twenty sections.

Thinking of that made him angry. He was angry because he had to hang around town and let a good deal slip away while some sheriff—appointed to serve until a new county could organize an election—tried to solve a murder mystery.

And what could he do about it? Just stand around and wait?

John McCrea reached a decision. He was no lawman and he knew nothing about solving crimes, but he couldn't just do nothing. He would ask some questions on his own.

He went back to Johnson's Corrals, made certain his two bay horses were well fed and hunted up Johnson. The stableman was thin and stoop-shouldered with a walrus moustache. He pushed his hat back and scratched his bald head when McCrea asked him about Old Levi.

"Wa-al, I sold 'im them two mules and some saddles. He paid with gold dust. We weighed it at The Palace so I know I got my money's worth. That's all I know."

"What kind of man was he? Did he talk at all?"

"Not much. And when he did he didn't always make sense. Tell you the truth, I think he was kinder tetched in the head."

"I guess you knew when he left town."

"Shore, I knew. He kept them mules here, and I seen 'im saddle 'em up and ride out of town."

"Did anybody else see him?"

"Shore. He went north around town like he didn't want anybody to see 'im, but there's too many people all around here. Somebody had to've seen 'im."

"Did you see anybody follow him?"

"Naw. But I wasn't watchin' 'im. I always got work to do, and I always mind my own business."

"Excuse me for asking so many questions, but did anybody else see him getting ready to ride out?"

"Had to. I keep maybe thirty hosses here, and there's always somebody here besides me."

"Do you remember who all was here when he saddled his mules?"

The stableman pulled at the end of his moustache with his right hand and looked down thoughtfully. "Just some miners, some prospectors. I don't know who they was."

"Then somebody did see him getting ready to leave town?"

"Shore. Had to've."

"Let me ask you one more question. Did anybody know which way he would be going?"

"Shore. Most folks knew that. When he left here before he went east and then north toward that mountain up there, that Squaw Mountain."

"And yet nobody knew where his find was?"

"There's a tolerable lot of country up there, mister." The stableman shook his head sadly. "A powerful lot of country. I'm bettin' nobody'll ever find that mine."

McCrea walked back to Main Street with his head down, lost in thought. Nobody was seen following Old Levi, but plenty of men knew he was leaving and which way he would be going. Somebody had gone ahead of him and waylaid him. The road going east carried a lot of traffic. It was the road to San Lomah, the old county seat. The Diamond J headquarters was about twenty miles east, and the wagons were seven or eight miles east.

And, let's see, the mine owned by Arkansas Henessy was just east of town. Henessy was no killer. No, not him. He had a rich mine of his own. What else was to the east? There were diggings in all directions.

Without thinking about where he was going, McCrea walked down Main Street heading east. Soon he found himself out of town and across the road from Arkansas Henessy's mine. An unpainted clapboard shack stood near the new steam engine, and men were gathered around the engine, tinkering with it. One of them was Arkansas Henessy. He looked up as McCrea approached.

"Mornin', son," he said. "Change yer mind about a job? I could use a good teamster."

As he approached, McCrea saw a hand-painted sign over the door of the shack. It said, Marylou Mine.

"No. Not yet, anyhow. But if I have to stay around here much longer I might change my mind."

Arkansas Henessy pulled a sack of Bull Durham out of a pocket in the bib of his baggy overalls and offered it to McCrea. "Set and smoke a spell."

McCrea took the offered makings and rolled a smoke. He lifted his right foot, bent his knee to tighten the rough denim of his pants' leg and struck a match on the outside of his thigh. He lit his smoke, shook the match, held it clasped in his hand for a few seconds to make sure it was out and dropped it.

Arkansas Henessy tamped tobacco into his corncob pipe and struck a match on a button of his suspenders. "Now ta make the mornin' brighter, how 'bout a drink of whiskey?"

McCrea didn't want a drink but he didn't want to turn down an offer from Henessy, either. "A short snort never hurt anybody."

"Come on in the shack."

Inside the one-room board building, furnished with two chairs, a small wood-burning stove, and a wooden table, Henessy poured whiskey from a quart bottle into two shot glasses and handed one to the cowboy. "I don't allow boozin' on the job, but we ain't neither one of us on the job now." He drank his whiskey in one swallow. McCrea did likewise.

"Just awalkin' fer yer health?"

"Not exactly. I guess you heard why I'm staying in town. I'd like to find out for myself who killed that old prospector. I was thinking he had to have come by here, and I was wondering if you or any of your men saw anybody following him."

"I seen 'im aridin' by on one mule and aleadin' another'n, but I didn't see airy soul acomin' along behind."

"Did you see anybody going east ahead of him?"

"Well shore. There was a whole string of freight wagons aheadin' fer San Lomah, and there was a coupla miners aheadin' for the old Badger Mine."

"The Badger Mine?"

"Yup. That's the one that eastern financyoor bought. You know, that Amos Tarr."

"Is that east of here?"

"'Bout four mile. An' if you ask me, there ain't nothin' in it but hard granite."

"What makes you think so?"

"I know Old Bertram Smith, and if he said the vein petered out it petered out."

"Is that the man Amos Tarr bought the mine from?"

"Yup, an' he's forgot more about gold minin' than that dandy'll ever know."

"Did you see Tarr that morning?"

Henessy answered with, "How 'bout another'n?" He picked up the bottle and poured two more drinks. "This'll cut the rust out of yer pipes. Yup, I seen 'im aridin' out to his mine, awearin' that long coat and that beaver hat and acarryin' that fancy rifle of his'n."

"Was he alone?"

"He was about a mile behind his two miners."

"Anybody else?"

"There was the high shurff of Justin County. He looked like he was agoin' prospectin'. An' there was a lot of other traffic agoin' up and down this road. I never paid no mind to most of it."

"I see." McCrea studied his whiskey glass.

"That financyoor saved yer life last night, I hear."

"He sure did. I don't know where that mule skinner got his gun, but he was about to shoot me full of holes."

"Didn't like ol' Wheeler the first time I saw 'im, but good help is hard to find around here. 'Nother snort?"

"No thanks. It's too early to get drunk. Guess I'll mosey back to town."

The two men left the shack and watched a tank wagon pull up to the steam engine. McCrea read the sign above the shack door aloud. "Marylou Mine. Marylou must be somebody you know."

"My wife of thutty year. We been poor all our lives and now we're rich. I sent for 'er, and when she gets here I'm agonna build 'er the biggest and finest house money can buy."

McCrea grinned. "That's the kind of story I like to hear."

Back at The Palace, McCrea ordered a beer, not because he wanted to drink it but because he wanted to pump the bartender for information. He had learned from experience that bartenders heard all the news and rumors.

"Did you know Old Levi?"

The bartender, a middle-aged bald man, rolled his left shirt sleeve up a little higher. "Nobody knew him. He hung around here sometimes but he never said much, just asked for whiskey and paid for it with dust or a nugget."

"Were you here when he came down from the mountain last winter?"

"Mister, I been here since Old Yip was a pup. Yeah, I saw him come tramping down the street, looking like he was half froze."

"Pardon my questions, but I guess you heard the sheriff thinks I might have had something to do with his murder, and I'd like to know more about him. What do you think? Do you think he killed his partner up there somewhere?"

"Yeah, I heard about you. You're lucky you ain't in the lockup at San Lomah. Old Harv would've put them fancy handcuffs on you last night if it wasn't for your long-tall friend."

"Yeah, I guess I owe Amos Tarr for my freedom too. What do you know abut Old Levi?"

"All I know is he went up there somewhere with a partner, a man from the East somewhere, and two mules and came back afoot and alone with all the gold he could carry."

"And he offered no explanation?"

"Not a word. Whoever bushwhacked him must be half Indian. A pair of toughies tried to follow him up to his mine last spring, and he made plumb fools out of 'em."

McCrea took a swallow of the beer. It was warm and tasted bitter. "What did the sheriff do about it?"

"We didn't have a sheriff then, except for Old Ben Taylor over at San Lomah, and he came over and asked

Old Levi a bunch of questions and left."

The bartender went to serve another customer and came back. "Some folks think he murdered his partner, but nobody can prove it. The new sheriff, Old Harv, took some men and went up toward Squaw Peak last spring and didn't find anything. Believe me, I tried to pump him for a hint of where his mine is, but he just dummied up. Say." He squinted at McCrea. "They say he was still alive when you found him. Did he say anything?"

"Nothing." McCrea finished his beer and turned to leave. "He tried to talk but he couldn't."

The bartender stared at McCrea's back for a long moment as if he didn't know whether to believe him.

Chapter Nine

The day that had started with a cool wind but bright sunshine had now turned cloudy and dark. Lightning flashed through the sky and thunder rumbled over to the west. McCrea went to Johnson's Corrals, picked up his warbag and carried it to the cot house. He unpacked his straight razor and used the washroom to shave. He wished he had a bath and some clean clothes. The clean clothes would be no problem. He could buy some. He needed new clothes anyway. But the bath was something else.

The cot house proprietor grunted when McCrea asked about bathing facilities and answered with, "If you want a bath you have to go to the hotel. There ain't no place to take a bath here. And you owe me twenty cents for usin' my washroom to shave."

McCrea went to the town's one dry goods store and bought some new cotton pants, a blue cotton shirt, socks, and underclothes. He knew the hotel was filled up, and it would be useless to even ask about taking a bath there, so he went to Johnson's Corrals, saddled one of his horses, a short-backed bay gelding, and rode south out of town, following a creek.

He rode three miles before he came to a place where the creek was screened by willows, and there he hobbled his horse, stripped and bathed. It was a cold bath, but it was the kind of bath he had taken a thousand times in his life. By the time he had finished, the rain was slanting down from the north, and lightning was cutting a fiery, jagged line on the ridge north of town. McCrea swore good-naturedly. "Hell, if I'd waited, I'd have got washed just riding."

It was a cold rain, and McCrea was reminded again that he was in a cold climate, and he was thankful that he had bought his heavy duck jacket in San Lomah before he started working for the Diamond J.

Back on the streets of Bluebird, McCrea was walking to the sheriff's office when he met Crystal Lee Brown. She had seen him coming, and it was too late to avoid her.

"Mr. McCrea," she said smiling, "nice to see you." The smile vanished and a frown creased her forehead. "Your poor face. I heard about the fight. I'm so glad you weren't seriously injured. You ought to do something for those abrasions."

"Aw." He grinned, feeling embarrassed. "They're a long way from any vital organs. They'll heal."

"They will heal quicker with medication. Come back to the cafe with me. I have some salve that will help."

"Aw, I don't need anything. Thanks just the same." He shuffled his feet. "I, uh, hope you don't get the wrong idea about me, Miss Brown. I usually stay out of fights, but this time I couldn't have run away if I'd wanted to."

"I know. I heard about it." She took his arm. "Come back to the cafe with me and let me play nurse. I've had some training for this sort of thing."

His protests failed to put her off, and finally he gave in. He sat in a straight-back wooden chair in the kitchen while her soft fingers worked on his face. He could smell the good, clean woman smell of her, see the tenderness in her eyes, feel her cool breath on his cheek. Lordy, he thought, what a man wouldn't do for a woman like this. A man would go to hell for a woman like this.

Just before sundown he went back to the sheriff's office and found Sheriff G.B. Harvey sitting with his feet propped up, reading a pulp magazine.

"No," Harvey said and sighed. "I haven't heard one damn thing that's new."

"Listen, sheriff, I've been asking around, and it looks like everybody in Bluebird knew Old Levi had a rich find somewhere, and probably two dozen men knew he was leaving town and which way he would be going. That makes a hell of a lot of men who could have followed him or gone ahead and waylaid him."

McCrea paused for breath. "Now if you are a reasonable man, you'll admit that any one of two dozen men are just as suspect as I am, and I can go on my way. I could stay around town here forever. You might never find out who killed that old man."

The sheriff's feet hit the floor. "Now you listen, young fella, if I'd locked you up like I should have, there wouldn't have been that killing last night. You'll stay here and you'll keep out of trouble or you'll sure as hell end up in the hoosegow."

McCrea said nothing more, except, "Well, I'm reporting like you said to do."

"Get on out of here. And you'd better stay out of that saloon."

He waited until most of the crowd had left the Bluebird Cafe and went back and sat at the counter. After he had eaten he offered to wash dishes, but Crystal Lee told him she had a dishwasher now, a man sent over by Amos Tarr.

"He evidently knows where to look to hire people," she said. "We are certainly glad to have the help."

"When is Amos Tarr going to take over?"

"In a day or two. He said he sent to Denver for a cook, but he is going to keep Maudie on, too. He said there will be enough business for two cooks, and he is probably right."

McCrea was disappointed. He had hoped to spend more time in her kitchen, getting better acquainted. But on second thought, nothing could come of it. He was trouble. No woman needed the kind of trouble he would bring.

He waited until he was outside on the plank sidewalk before he grumbled to himself. "Dammit all anyway." His boots clomped on the planks, and his spur rowels rang like tiny bells as he walked away, shaking his head sadly, thinking of Crystal Lee Brown.

As before, he carried his bedroll out of town a short distance and unrolled it at the bottom of a grassy hill. He lay on top of the tarp for a time, looking at the stars and thinking. When the terrible memory came back, he had a strong urge to get up and go back to The Palace. Maybe whiskey would drive the memory away. His dad, dying, blood bubbling out of his mouth. The saloon, gunshots, three men down, the miracle of being still alive. The reputation. Men talking behind his back. Young toughs looking him over, wondering if they could kill him in a shootout and win a reputation for themselves. It was impossible to live peacefully there. Ride. Get far away.

Whiskey would help.

Whiskey would not help. His dad had repeatedly preached to him about that. Take a friendly drink now and then, sure, but don't turn to the bottle to solve a problem. Whiskey only makes it worse.

Finally, McCrea pulled off his boots and pants and crawled between the blankets. He forced himself to think of other things. Crystal Lee Brown. Now there's a woman a man could build to. Pretty, intelligent, always smiling. But troubled. Yes, he had seen trouble in her eyes. Wonder what her trouble is. Seems everybody has troubles.

John McCrea finally drifted off to sleep. He was dreaming a troubled dream when he was awakened by the sound of a gun being cocked close to his head.

He awoke with a start and jerked upright only to be knocked down again by a blow to the head. Bright lights shot through his brain as he fell back, and a voice muttered, "One wrong move and you're a dead man."

"What?" That was all McCrea could say. He squinted in the darkness, trying to find the voice. He made out a vague shape of a man standing over him. The man was pointing a six-gun at his face. Another voice came from behind him. "Get on your feet and move mighty slow."

"Who—who are you?" McCrea's voice was unsteady. His head hurt.

"Shut your trap. Don't say nothin'. Get up."

McCrea folded the blanket and tarp away from his legs and got his feet out of the bed. Now he could make out two men, one in front of him and another to his right. Both had six-guns. He looked up at the sky. The stars were out, seemingly so low he could almost reach up and touch them, but there was no moon.

"Pull on your boots. You're goin' for a walk."

He reached for his boots and pants, which he kept at the foot of his mattress inside the folded-over bed tarp. He pulled the boots on first, cowboy style, so that when he stood to pull on his pants he was not standing in his bare feet. He tried to make out the features of the two men, but the darkness hid their faces.

Fully dressed, he calculated his chances of escape. Not good. Two guns were pointed at him from different directions.

"All right, on your belly."

"Listen," McCrea said, "I don't know you. What do you want? Who are you?"

"You'll find out. Hit the dirt. Right now, or I'll knock you down."

McCrea lay on his stomach on top of the bed. He kept his head turned toward the men, still trying to get a better look at them.

"Put your hands behind your back." McCrea did as he was told. His hands were jerked further back, and his wrists were tied with a grass rope. "On your feet." He tried to turn his wrists and was unable to do so. They were tied tight. A rough hand grabbed him by the hair and half pulled him to his feet. A fist hit him on the jaw. "You move when I tell you to or you'll die right here."

The blow made McCrea gasp. "Why? Who are you? Are you lawmen?"

A guffaw came from one of the men. "Lawmen? I've been called a lot of names but not lawman."

"Go get the horses," the other man said.

A grumble came from the second man and he growled, "You sure like to give orders." McCrea saw his shape fade away into the darkness.

The other man stayed in front of him. "This pistol is loaded and cocked," he said in a warning tone.

With his hands tied behind his back, McCrea was almost helpless. His only hope was to try to run in the dark. If he could get forty feet away, they would have a hard time finding him. He glanced around, looking for a boulder or a clump of brush or anything to head for. All he could see was blackness.

"Don't try it." There was a deadly menace in the man's voice. "One move and I'll fill you full of .45 slugs."

Soon more shapes appeared, and McCrea could hear the shod hoofs of horses striking the rocks. The man leading them stepped in front of McCrea and slipped a loop over his head, down his back and up again under his tied hands, up to his armpits. The loop was pulled tight around his chest.

Saddle leather creaked as the two men mounted. One of the horses was nervous and the rider swore, "Damn hammerhead."

"All right," a man said, "you're goin' for a walk. I mean you're goin' for a run. Keep up or I'll drag you."

A hard jerk on the rope around his chest brought McCrea to his knees. "Get up." He got up and another jerk forced him forward. He walked, trying to keep up with the pull on the rope. He knew the other end of the rope was wrapped around a saddle horn. He had to keep his feet moving to keep from being jerked down and dragged. He walked, stumbled over a rock, kept his balance and broke into a running walk behind the horses. The rope was constantly pulling, threatening to jerk him down on his face in the dirt and rocks.

Chapter Ten

It was another sleepless night for Crystal Lee Brown. What she feared most had happened. It had happened at suppertime, after most of the customers had paid and left. Two men had stayed behind, smirking at her. Then when she started to pick up the dirty dishes in front of them, one of them grabbed her by the wrist. When she tried to pull back, he said, "Don't be so uppity, whore."

The other man laughed. "What do you charge nowadays? More than in Dallas, I'll bet."

"How much to go back to that cabin with you?"

Both men laughed wickedly.

Crystal Lee remembered what she had been taught long ago about how to free herself from a man's grasp, and she twisted her wrist against his thumb. It hurt, but she broke free and ran to the kitchen. Maudie saw the fear and revulsion in her face.

"What happened, Miss Brown? Did somebody bother you, hon?" Maudie grabbed a butcher knife and headed for the dining room. "Let me at 'em. They cain't treat you that way."

"No Maudie. They've got guns. Don't go in there." Crystal Lee grabbed the back of Maudie's dress and tried to restrain her. The new dishwasher, a short man with a humped back, grabbed a meat cleaver and headed for the dining room, too.

"What did they do, Miss Brown? Did they hurt you?"

"No," Crystal Lee answered. "Don't. They're leaving. They didn't hurt me."

The two men got up and walked to the front door, hawhawing. One of them, a man with a scar on his right cheek, looked back at the two women and the disfigured dishwasher. He put his hand on the butt of the pistol he carried on his right hip. "That's some army you got there, Miss Texas whore. Haw-haw." They left.

Crystal Lee did something then that she had vowed she would not do. She couldn't help it. She broke into tears. Maudie put a heavy black arm around her, led her to the work table and got her to sit. "There, there, honey. Don't let 'em bother you. You're a nice lady. I don't care what they say. You're a nice lady."

The dishwasher stood helplessly by wanting to do something. Finally, he said, "You're a princess, Miss Brown."

She had to leave, Crystal Lee decided later, while she lay awake in her cabin. She couldn't wait for the new bank to open. She had already accepted Amos Tarr's note, and now she would have to leave and hope she could convert it to cash later. Where would she go? California? Yes, she would go as far west as she could, to the edge of the continent. Fortunately, she had not invested everything in the Bluebird Cafe and she had money. And she could get a job. She was a good bookkeeper, and she knew how to run a kitchen. Those were things Aunt Agnes had taught her. She could always earn a living.

Perhaps she could find a new life on the West Coast. Perhaps—perhaps she could even find a good man to share the rest of her life with. If she did, should she tell him? It was a question Crystal Lee had wrestled with before. She groaned aloud. "What should I do?"

Her heart leaped into her throat when she heard the knock on the door. She got up and slipped a wool robe on over her nightdress. "Who is it?" she asked, her voice fearful.

There was no answer.

Fear took hold of her then, and she trembled with it. She screamed when the door was rammed open, splitting the doorjamb. Her scream was cut off abruptly when a rough, callused hand was clamped over her mouth.

Twice, John McCrea fell face down, and both times it felt as if his face were being scraped raw. Strangely, he missed the hat he had been forced to leave with his bed. The hat would have given his face some protection. He went on, half pulled in a running walk that he thought would never end. He tried to reason with the men, but they were not listening. When he stumbled and fell the third time, he managed to twist his body so that he fell on his left shoulder, and from there he flipped onto his back. It was less painful that way, being dragged on the seat of his pants, and it even allowed him a short minute's rest. But the man stopped the horse and ordered him back onto his feet.

Once, the horse that was not pulling him spooked at something in the dark and nearly threw its rider. The rider swore. "Goddamn hammerhead. Always lookin' for somethin' to booger at." The other man chuckled. "Old Johnson saw you comin' when he sold you that brute. Give him a chance and he'll throw your ass off and head for home."

"If he does, I'll shoot him and that goddamn Johnson, too."

They went on in silence, McCrea trying desperately to keep up and stay on his feet. His legs felt as if they were carrying lead weights instead of feet, and he wondered how much farther he could go before they collapsed.

Finally, they crossed a creek where McCrea fell again and got sopping wet, went around a pile of huge boulders and stopped. "All right, cowboy, here's where the ball begins. If you think you've been treated rough, you ain't seen nothin' yet."

The two men dismounted and one of them shoved McCrea back against a boulder. "Set right there and don't move a muscle."

"Why? What have I done to you?"

"Don't talk either or I'll lay your head open with a gun barrel."

The other man shivered audibly and said he was going to try to find some firewood. McCrea heard him stumble over a rock, swear, and shuffle around, groping for something to burn. He heard him break limbs off a tree and remembered that the lower limbs of mountain pines were dead because the sun couldn't reach them. The man came up, broke the limbs into small pieces and struck a match. He cursed when the wood didn't burn and the match went out. But he struck another match and this time got a small flame going.

Soon a fire was crackling not far from McCrea's feet, and he was grateful for it. The high altitude air was cold and he was wet, and the fire felt good. It also gave him an opportunity to study the faces of the two men.

They were nobody he had ever seen before. One was of medium height, thickset, with a clean-shaven, beefy face. The other was short and lean with a sharp face and constantly shifting eyes. He wore a wide leather belt lined with silver Mexican conches that glittered in the firelight. When he stood, he tilted sharply to the right, favoring his right leg which was several inches shorter than the other. Like a cornered coyote, he appeared ready to spring and snap at anything.

Both men carried six-guns tied low on their right thighs, and the short, lean crippled man carried a bowie knife in a leather sheath in his left hip. McCrea guessed the short man to be the most dangerous one.

They squatted near the fire, smoked cigarettes and soaked up its warmth. McCrea sat with his back to the high boulder and said nothing. Slowly, the sky to the east brightened. McCrea's bound hands had ached at first, but now they felt numb. The brightening sky revealed the two horses standing tied to a tree nearby and a small half circle of boulders around them.

McCrea's captors smoked cigarette after cigarette until visibility was fairly good, then the short one stood up and threw more wood on the fire. He pulled on a pair of cowhide gloves and limped over to McCrea.

"It's time," he said. He jerked the bowie knife free. "Stand up.'"

McCrea tried to stand. He got halfway up but his legs buckled, and he fell in a heap. The short man nearly fell over, but he managed to kick McCrea in the ribs. "Try again." McCrea rolled until he could get his feet under him, and this time he straightened and stayed up. "Hold him," the cripple said.

"Still givin' orders, ain't you," the other man grumbled.

Strong hands grabbed McCrea from behind, grabbed his dark hair and pulled his head back. He felt a sharp point against the side of his neck.

"What you feel, cowboy, is a razor-sharp steel blade. Now if you don't say what we want you to say, I'm gonna slit your throat and you're gonna die chokin' on your own blood."

"What—" McCrea fought to keep his voice under control. "What do you want?"

"You know what we want. Gold. Now I'm gonna ask you once and once only. What did that old prospector tell you?"

"Nothing." McCrea couldn't keep the fear out of his voice. "It's like I told the sheriff, like I told everybody, he died before he could say anything."

A sharp pain stabbed at the side of his neck, and he knew he had been cut. The short cripple chuckled without mirth. "That's just a nick. Next time I'm gonna cut deeper. Now, what did he tell you?"

"I told you. He couldn't talk. I'm not lying."

Another sharp pain and another cruel chuckle. "Keep that up and you're gonna be cut to pieces a little at a time." McCrea tried to think, to gather his wits about him. "Listen, if I knew where that mine is I'd be up there, wouldn't I? I'm telling you I don't know."

"You know. You was seen cuttin' the ropes off that old man. You didn't know it but you was bein' watched. The old man's mouth moved. He told you, all right. He knew he was dyin', and he told you."

McCrea's head was held back so far he had to look down his nose to see the short man. "You're the one," he said. "You're the one the sheriff is looking for."

The cruel chuckle came again. "What're you gonna do about it?"

"It was the two of you. Listen," McCrea wanted to reason with them. "The sheriff told me he died of a heart attack. You didn't kill him. Maybe it wasn't murder. You're not murderers yet. Killing me won't get you anything." As soon as he said it he knew he was wasting his breath. The man behind him grunted and yanked his head back further.

"Let me have the knife. I know how to cut a man's face muscles so his features run in a pool."

"No, you just hold him. We know the old man told him something."

The hold on McCrea's hair relaxed a trifle. "I don't know what happened up there but I want the gold as bad as you and the boss."

"Shut up," the cripple hissed. "I'm in charge here."

The hold on McCrea's hair was suddenly released. "The hell you are." The husky man stepped around between McCrea and the cripple. "What makes you think you're so goddamn important?"

"That's what he said. He told me to take charge here

and find out what this cowpuncher knows."

"The hell he did. We'll see about that." The husky man stomped away toward the horses. "I'm tired of bein' treated like a goddamn flunky."

"Where the hell are you goin'?"

"To town. See what he says to my face. You stay here with him. I'll be back and maybe I'll bring the boss back with me."

"You crazy bastard."

"What did you say?" The husky man turned back and stood straddle-legged, his hand over the butt of his gun.

For a moment they glared at each other. The short one straightened, standing on his left foot, ready for a gunfight. "Go on, go for your gun." His voice was cold, deadly. "Go ahead."

McCrea sidestepped out of the thickset one's line of fire. Silently, he wished they would shoot. Maybe they would shoot each other. But then the thickset man dropped his hands and turned back to the horses. He spoke over his shoulder. "We'll just see what the boss says about this."

He jerked the reins from a tree limb, and the sudden movement caused the brown horse he had freed to rear back and try to break away. The man swore. "You hammerheaded sonofabitch." The horse backed away and almost backed over the fire.

By the time the man got it stopped, it was standing, quivering, a few feet from McCrea.

Gathering the reins, the thickset man started to put his foot in the stirrup. The horse stood with its head up, quivering, ears twitching, watching the man.

John McCrea had handled his share of broncs, and he

knew that with a little encouragement this horse would blow the plug and buck like a scalded ape. He could tell, also, that the thickset man did not know how to handle broncs. The man held the reins loosely in his left hand, got hold of the saddle horn with his right hand and stuck his foot in the stirrup.

McCrea acted at the same instant the idea came to him. He took one long step forward and kicked the ground with the side of his foot. His kick threw a piece of firewood and a puff of dirt under the horse. That gave the animal the excuse it was looking for.

The horse let out a squeal, dropped its head and went straight up. At the top of the leap, its head came up and its heels snapped skyward. The rider turned a complete somersault eight feet above the ground and came down heavily on the flat of his back. The horse went on, hitting the ground every ten feet, empty stirrups flapping over the saddle. The crippled man was watching.

In two more running steps, McCrea rammed his head into the short man's stomach, knocking him flat, and before he could even start to rise, McCrea took a jump, twisted his body in midair and landed with the seat of his pants on the man's chest. Breath whooshed out of the man's lungs and a rib cracked.

McCrea bounced up and down on him twice more to make sure he was out cold, then looked for the knife. He saw it on the ground only a few feet away.

The brown horse was still pitching, and the other horse, startled at the excitement, had broken the reins it was tied with and was running in the opposite direction.

McCrea scooted on the seat of his pants to the knife and got his tied hands on it. Watching the two men, he tried by feel to turn the knife blade toward him, to where it would cut the ropes. Instead, it cut the top of one wrist. McCrea tried again.

The short man was groaning. The other man was beginning to pick himself up, slowly and painfully.

Hastily, McCrea began moving the knife back and forth, hoping that it would come into contact with the rope. Finally, he felt it working on the rope, and then he was free.

He stood up and rubbed his bleeding wrists. Flexing his fingers, he went first to the thickset man who was sitting up, shaking his head groggily. He grabbed the gun from the man's holster and brought the barrel down hard on the man's head just above the left ear. The thickset man fell back and lay still.

Next, McCrea went to the other man, took his gun and stuck it in the waist of his pants. The short man was groaning, struggling to rise. McCrea grabbed him by the front of his shirt and pulled him to a sitting position, then squatted in front of him and pointed a gun at his face. McCrea grinned without humor.

"Now tell me something you sonofabitch, just who in the hell is your boss?"

The gunman mumbled, "Go to hell."

McCrea continued grinning. "I'm a killer, didn't you hear? I've killed men before." The short man groaned again. "Too bad about your ribs," McCrea said. "I've seen broken ribs that punctured a lung, causing a man to die a slow painful death."

"Aw shit."

"You men gave me hell and I'm going to give it back to you unless you tell me who your boss is."

The gunman raised his head. "What'll you do if I tell you?"

"Let you live."

"Will you give me my horse and let me leave the country?"

"Nope." McCrea shook his head. "I need you to tell the sheriff what happened to Old Levi. He thinks I might have done it."

The gunman's lips turned up in a sneer. "My heart bleeds for you."

The grin left McCrea's face and his features turned hard. "Who is your boss?"

"Go to hell."

The gun was only inches from the man's face. McCrea's finger tightened on the trigger. He had been led behind a horse until his legs had turned rubbery. He had been dragged. He had been hit, kicked, and cut with a knife. He was justified in killing this man. In fact, he would be doing the world a favor.

But instead, he relaxed his trigger finger and stood up. "Pull off your boots."

"What?"

"Your boots. Pull them off or I'll shoot off your right ear and your left ear and your nose. Do it."

Moving slowly, the man pulled off the left boot, then the right one. McCrea picked them up with his left hand. "Now your pants." The man had to stand, tilted, to take his pants off, but he did as McCrea ordered. "Sit down and don't move."

McCrea went to the fire, fed it some wood and then fed it the boots and pants. He went to the thickset man who was still unconscious and pulled off his boots and pants.

The man wore no underclothes. McCrea pitched them into the fire and watched until they were reduced to charcoal.

Then he went looking for the horses.

The gentle horse was nowhere in sight, but the brown bronc had stopped bucking and was standing with its head down and its sides heaving. "You'll have to do," McCrea said as he walked to the horse on rubbery legs.

Chapter Eleven

The brown horse watched McCrea approach but made no attempt to turn away. It raised its head and snorted when the cowboy picked up the reins.

"You've had your fun for the day, old pony, and you probably saved my life. I won't be hard on you."

McCrea took the left rein in his left hand and with the same hand got hold of the horse's mane. He turned his hand upside down, grasping a hank of mane, and twisted his wrist so that the left rein was tightened. The horse backed a step to relieve the pressure on its mouth, and McCrea relaxed his hold. "If you jump, old pony, you're gonna have to jump toward me, not away from me."

Cautiously, he took the right rein and the saddle horn in his right hand and put his foot in the stirrup. He pushed his knee solidly against the horse's shoulder and started up. The bronc had bucked off one man and was ready to do it again. It snorted and jumped, trying to get its head down to buck.

McCrea twisted his wrist and the hank of mane, tightening the left rein, keeping the horse's head up.

With his knee against the animal's shoulder, one hand on the saddle horn and the other grasping the mane, he was able to brace himself and ride it out, hanging onto the horse's side.

The horse took two shallow jumps and when it paused, McCrea swung his right foot over its rump and into the stirrup on the off side. He let go his hold on the mane and took both reins in his left hand. The horse went to bucking in earnest.

Instead of pulling on the saddle horn, the cowboy pushed on it to keep from being thrown over the horse's head. The horse squalled and pitched, but McCrea had worked on horseback all his life, and many times he had worked from the backs of horses that were anything but gentle.

When the horse slowed its bucking, he whipped it with the end of the reins, got it into a gallop and turned it toward town.

He rode into town from the west, stopped to pick up the hat he had lost the night before, rode past Johnson's Corrals and down the street to the sheriff's office, still at a gallop. He pulled the horse to a stop in front of the sheriff's log cabin of an office and tied it with the reins to a hitch rack. The office was closed, and McCrea stopped a passing miner and asked where the sheriff lived. He mounted the bronc again, this time by grabbing the headstall with his left hand and pulling the horse's head toward him.

Sheriff G.B. Harvey lived in a frame house a quarter mile from his office. The house had been freshly painted white. McCrea tied the horse to a hitch rail in front of a white picket fence, walked to the front door and knocked.

A gray, middle-aged, hard-faced woman answered.

"No, he had to go over to San Lomah, and he left just after daylight." She frowned. "What happened to your face? Have you been fighting?"

"No, uh, well yes, uh—"

"You're that Johnny McCrea, aren't you?" Her glance took in the pistol carried inside McCrea's waistband. "And you're carrying a gun."

"Mrs. Harvey, I've got a problem and I don't know what to do about it." He tried to ignore her accusing look. "I left two men about four miles west of town without boots or pants, and one of them had a hand in killing Old Levi."

"Is that so?" She said it accusingly, and McCrea knew she did not believe him. "And I'm not Mrs. Harvey. I'm his housekeeper."

He looked down at his boots, trying to decide what to do. "Well, when the sheriff gets back will you tell him what I said? I'm going to try to bring those two men to town and hold them somewhere until he gets back."

For the third time, he mounted the bronc. The horse was too tired now to do any fighting, and it trotted obediently down the street. When he approached the Bluebird Cafe, McCrea saw a group of men standing by the front door, and Maudie, wringing her hands and crying. Maudie saw him and cried out to him. "Oh Mr. McCrea, somethin' turrible's happened."

McCrea dismounted and led the bronc to the front door. "What's happened, Maudie? What's wrong?"

Tears ran down Maudie's strong black face. "It's Miss Brown. Somethin's happened. I went to her cabin when she didn't show up this mornin' and the door was smashed in. Somethin' turrible's happened, Mr. McCrea."

Fear leaped into McCrea's throat and a chill went up his back. His question came out in a hoarse whisper. "She's gone?"

"She's gone, Mr. McCrea. Somethin's happened."

The cowboy's intestines twisted into a knot. "Show me." Still leading the bronc, he followed the plump black woman around the corner of the Bluebird Cafe to the alley and to Crystal Lee Brown's cabin. A half-dozen men followed. It was as Maudie had said: The door was standing open and the doorjamb was splintered.

McCrea groaned aloud. "Oh Lord, they've got her, too."

"She's gone, Mr. McCrea." Tears were spilling from Maudie's eyes. "Somebody done kidnapped her. Poor Miss Brown."

"Listen, Maudie." McCrea took the black woman by the shoulders. "Listen. I think I know which way they went. The sheriff's out of town now, and when he gets back, I want you to tell him something. Will you do that?"

"I shorely will."

"Tell him I think they went east with her. I was kidnapped, too, but I got away and I just came in from the west. I think they went east and I'm going after them. Will you tell him that, Maudie?"

"I shorely will, Mr. McCrea."

McCrea stepped onto the brown horse and took off at a gallop toward Johnson's Corrals. Maudie watched him go and whispered, "May the Lord ride with you, Mr. McCrea."

McCrea stepped off the brown horse before it came to a stop, tossed the reins at Johnson and yelled, "Take care of him." He ran to the harness room, grabbed his own saddle, blanket, and bridle and hurried to the corrals where he caught and saddled one of his own horses. He started to mount, then went back to the harness room to his warbag. He rummaged through it until he found his old Colt .44 and the holster and belt. He buckled it on.

Johnson watched him curiously. "You goin' bear huntin' or somethin'?"

"Yeah." With that, McCrea mounted and rode away at a gallop, heading east out of town.

G.B. Harvey's housekeeper was sweeping the front porch when he galloped past. She stopped what she was doing, watched until he was out of sight and shook her head sadly. "Too bad," she said to herself. "He's probably a nice-looking young man when his face isn't skinned up, but he'll end up in a hangman's noose as sure as anything."

For the first few miles McCrea didn't look for tracks. Too many wagons and horses had gone over the road. But after he passed the last of the working mines, he slowed the horse to a trot and kept his eyes peeled for tracks leaving the road and going across country.

He was guessing that they had somehow forced the young woman onto a horse and were taking her somewhere away from town where they would have privacy. There they would force her to tell them everything Old Levi had told her. They would treat her the way the two gunmen had treated him, except that they were taking her in a different direction.

Judging from what McCrea's captors had said, somebody was bossing the scheme and probably had an organization behind him. Their scheme, McCrea guessed, was to get what information they could out of him, put that together with what they could get out of Miss Brown, and go hunting for the lost mine.

The thickset man had mentioned a "boss," and the short thin one had said somebody had put him in charge. Who was that somebody? Was he up ahead somewhere with Miss Brown as his captive? Would they cut her and beat her the way they did him? What would they do to her? A terrible urgency came over the cowboy.

He left the road where it crossed an open park and rode parallel to it but a hundred feet to the north. He guessed that they had eventually left the road and gone north toward Squaw Mountain. Everyone seemed to think the lost mine was somewhere around that snow-covered mountain, and McCrea had found the dying man far to the north of the road.

The bay horse was blowing hard from an uphill climb when McCrea finally saw the tracks. At first he could only make out an occasional mark on the ground and on the rocks where a shod horse had traveled. Only a shod hoof could scuff the rocks. McCrea knew that the Diamond J riders who worked that part of the country did not shoe their mounts. Each rider had as many as fourteen horses, and if they tried to keep them all shod, they would have had time for little else.

McCrea had seldom shod horses in the Pecos Valley of New Mexico, but he had bought shoes and nails, borrowed tools and shod his two horses when he first rode into the "Sangres" of Colorado.

Looking ahead, McCrea saw that the park ended at a thick forest of lodgepole pines, and he knew the ground there would be covered with fallen pine needles. He lifted the bay horse into a gallop again to the edge of the forest,

109

then slowed to a walk and studied the ground. He traveled parallel to the park about a hundred yards when he crossed their trail again. Dismounting, he took a closer look at the ground and guessed that three horses had left vague imprints and small tufts of overturned soil in the pine needles.

Tracking them through the lodgepoles was easy, and when he broke out into another small park, he was able to track them into a stand of aspens. McCrea had learned from experience that aspens grew fast and died fast, and wherever there was a stand of aspens, there was a lot of down timber. It was easy to see where the three horses had stepped over downed trees and onto small downed branches. Once out of the "Quakers," the tracks led into the tall spruce and ponderosa. Tracking from there on was slow.

But McCrea knew now which direction they were going, and he tried to look ahead and figure out where he would go if he were in their place, going toward Squaw Mountain. Twice, however, he outguessed himself and had to backtrack to pick up their trail. The second time, he followed their tracks across a shallow ravine and lost them again.

He was puzzled. He rode north from the ravine, guessing that his quarry was still going north, but when he failed to find their trail after a half mile, he had to go back. He was losing time, he knew, and he rode at a gallop back to the ravine. There, he finally picked up the trail again, this time staying with the tracks even though the going was slow. Finally, he felt like giving up.

By now the sun was straight overhead and a little to the south, and McCrea's stomach reminded him that he had not eaten since the night before. To hell with eating, he said to himself. He had to find them and keep them from hurting Miss Brown.

While he was following tracks, McCrea was looking ahead, trying to see a place where the trio would likely stop and do their dirty work. Trouble was the country was full of boulders, clumps of willows, and all kinds of places where men could hide what they were doing and where a woman's screams would not be heard.

McCrea knew that if they did not stop soon, and if he did not find them, they would be so far ahead he would lose their tracks in the dark. Repeatedly, he had to dismount and study the ground closely to stay on their trail.

It was mid-afternoon when he lost them. He circled back to where he had last seen the tracks and tried again to follow them. But the ground was too rocky, and to make matters worse Diamond J cattle had grazed here recently, and the marks they left were indistinguishable in the rocks from the marks the horses had made.

McCrea rode ahead, silently swearing, to the bottom of a long hill. He rode across the foot of the hill for two miles, hoping to cross the tracks there. When that failed, he rode around the hill, going far to the west of where he had guessed the trio was headed. Still he saw nothing that resembled horse tracks. But it was there that he saw the rider.

The rider was halfway up the same grassy, pine-studded hill that McCrea had crossed, and at first McCrea feared it was one of the kidnappers watching their back trail. But when the rider turned his horse downhill, McCrea recognized him.

The rider had seen McCrea and was coming down to meet him, and McCrea turned his horse uphill to meet

111

the rider halfway. They were still fifty feet apart when the rider grinned from beneath his long moustache and said, "Johnny. How's she goin'?"

"Howdy, Jud." McCrea reined up. His horse was blowing from the hard climb. "Seen anybody up this way today?"

"Naw. Ain't seen nobody or no cows neither. Why? Who're you lookin' for?" The Diamond J cow boss pushed his dirty white hat back on his head and wiped his forehead with a shirt sleeve.

"Two men and a woman," McCrea answered. There was an urgency in his voice and a tightness in his mouth that had Judson Olesky puzzled.

"What's wrong, Johnny? Somebody get lost? What happened to your face? Where's your hat?"

"It's important that I find them, Jud. At least one of them had a hand in killing that old prospector."

"That so?"

"Yeah. And the woman they've got with them is Crystal Lee Brown who owns the Bluebird Cafe. They've kidnapped her."

Olesky's mouth dropped open. "No. Why in hell'd they do that?"

McCrea spoke hurriedly, urgently. "They think the old prospector might have told her where his mine is, and they're going to force it out of her."

"Well fer—which way do you figger they went?"

"I can only guess. The old prospector was going north after he left the San Lomah road, and I'm guessing they went north, too, probably toward that mountain up there."

Olesky turned his horse around. "I'll go with you. I see you're packin' iron and I don't blame you, but two guns are better than one. Have you cut their sign?"

"I lost them back there about three miles. I don't know which way they went from there."

"Wa-al, let's see." Olesky tugged at one end of his moustache. "We got to think this out."

"Listen, Jud." McCrea was impatient, wanting to get back to his task. "You probably know this country better than any man alive. I'm guessing they will take her someplace where they can—" A lump came up in McCrea's throat. "Make her tell what she knows. If you were in their place where would you go?"

Olesky answered without hesitation. "To Shep's cabin."

"What? Where is that?"

"That is, Johnny, if they're in no hurry, and I reckon they ain't."

"Where is it, Jud?"

Olesky pointed with his right hand. "Over this hill there's a narrow crik that goes west a ways then north up a canyon. Up there is a grassy valley where Albert Trunsky used to keep his sheep in the summer. He built a cabin up there and stayed with 'em ever' summer 'til the snow flew, then threw 'em down on the flats."

"There's nobody there now?"

"Naw. Ain't been for five, six years. Trunsky, we all called him Shep, got out of the business. Lost too many of his flock to the coyotes. But I was up there three, four weeks ago, and that cabin is still standin'."

"And it's between here and that white peak?"

"Yup. A little to the west, but almost in line."

"That's where I'm going."

"I'll go with you."

"Wait, Jud. The best thing to do—the sheriff should

113

be coming along here tonight or early tomorrow morning. The best thing to do is find him and tell him where I went. I'm going to need him."

"Hell, maybe he can track us up there, Johnny."

"Maybe he can and maybe he can't. He doesn't strike me as being much of a tracker or anything else. No, you can help more by sending him in the right direction, Jud. And you can ride with him if he needs help."

The cow boss was used to giving orders, not taking them, but he could see the logic in McCrea's argument. Besides, his horse had been ridden hard since sunup and was tired. "All right, Johnny. But you'll never make it up there tonight. The trail up that canyon is a rough one, and you'll never make it in the dark."

McCrea lifted his reins and rode away at a fast trot. "I'll have to try."

Chapter Twelve

The climb up the long hill was a steep one, and McCrea had to stop three times and let his horse blow. The terrible sense of urgency was still with him, but he would not ride a horse to death. At the top of the hill he allowed the horse to stop again, and he studied the narrow valley below him.

He could see where a trickle of water ran through some willows for about four hundred yards, then wound through fifty or so acres of cinquefoil. Everything was turning yellow. The yellow willow leaves were mostly on the ground now, and the cinquefoil leaves were turning yellow brown and were dropping fast. Even the long clump grass was turning yellow.

Across the valley a small stand of aspens stood bare of leaves, telling McCrea that he had gained considerable altitude since leaving town and was in a different climate zone.

The sun was still sending down warmth, but McCrea guessed that when the sun went down, the temperature would drop twenty or thirty degrees.

He sent his bay gelding downhill, sliding at times, and at the bottom, he turned upstream. He had not gone more than a mile when he knew that Judson Olesky had guessed right. The tracks were there, three shod horses, also following the creek. But McCrea could tell by the color of the droppings from one of the horses that they were a good half day ahead. The sun had just gone down behind the western horizon when he came to where the creek poured out of a deep canyon.

McCrea paused and looked up the canyon, up at the sky, and then studied the canyon again. The creek carried more water in the canyon than it did in the valley, and McCrea guessed that it branched somewhere back in the willows. The fact that water was running swiftly in the creek made McCrea realize that snow was still melting somewhere uphill from him.

He urged his mount on. "Sorry, old pony, but I have to."

The trail was all uphill. It had for many decades been nothing more than a game trail. Then sheep and cattle had traveled over it, widening it. Cattle were good trail makers, but trampling hooves could not move boulders, and the trail was barely passable in places.

It was nearly dark when McCrea crossed the creek, rode around a pile of boulders, then back across the creek. He came to a pocket in the canyon wall and stopped. Looking up at the darkening sky, he spoke to the horse. "What do you think, old pony? Can we make it in the dark?"

The pocket went back about twenty feet, and water marks on the boulders told McCrea that it had once been under water. A flash flood had once sent water roaring down the canyon with enough force to move ton-sized boulders, piling them up and shoving them together in places.

Common sense told McCrea to stop here for the night. The grass was stirrup high in the pocket, and the horse could rest and eat his fill. But the terrible urgency would not leave him. That pretty Miss Brown was up there somewhere with two men who had kidnapped her. Anger mixed with the urgency, and McCrea rode on. "Those swine. Anybody that would pick on a woman is a dirty, mean, lowdown sonofabitch."

It was too dark now for McCrea to see the trail, and he had to depend upon the animal senses of his horse to follow it. McCrea had ridden horses in the dark many times, and he knew they had good night vision. And like all grazing animals, they would instinctively follow a trail.

It was pitch dark now and McCrea could see nothing, not even the horse's ears. All he could do was sit in the saddle and hope the animal managed to stay on its feet. At times he felt foolish. "I can't be much help to her if I'm on the bottom of the creek with a horse on top of me," he muttered. Later, he again apologized to the horse. "Get us up there, old pony, and I'll see that you get a good long rest."

Once, when the horse stopped, McCrea used his spurs to urge it on. A half hour later it stopped again. "Come on, old pony. We can't stop now. It can't be much farther to the top." He jerked on the reins of the horse, but it refused to go forward. He dug his spurs into the horse's sides, but instead of moving forward, the animal spun around on its hind feet and headed back the way it had come.

McCrea got it stopped and turned back. He urged it on

until it stopped again. "What in hell's the matter? What in hell's out there?"

The cowboy got down and lit a match. The night was as black as sin and not a breeze was stirring. McCrea made out a rock wall on his left and a huge boulder on his right, but he could see nothing ahead. The match burned down to his fingers, and he dropped it and lit another. Still, he could see nothing ahead. When that match burned his fingers, he lit a third one and tossed it out in front of him.

The lighted match dropped. And dropped. It fell a good fifteen feet before it went out.

"Good gawd almighty," McCrea whispered. "There's nothing there." He turned back and found the horse's head in the dark. He scratched the horse's neck. "Good boy. Good old pony. I'm sure sorry I mistreated you."

Staying on the ground, he turned the animal around. "We missed the trail somewhere along here," he said. "Where in hell does it go?"

He led the horse back the way they had come, walking slowly and carefully. Soon he heard running water to his left, and he knew they had met the creek again. Kneeling, he struck another match and studied the ground in the dim light. Six matches later and twenty feet downstream he found the tracks. "Yep. They crossed here. Here's where we go."

McCrea stepped into the saddle and urged the horse across the creek, then slacked up on the reins and let it pick its way again. "Don't know what made you lose the trail, old pony, but be careful, will you? My bones break easier than yours."

They crossed the creek several times, and each time McCrea could only tell by sound that they were in the water. The horse was tiring but responded to a light touch of the spurs. On they went, steel-shod hooves clattering over the rocks, sometimes striking sparks in the darkness. The horse's back swayed to the right and to the left. Most of the time the horse was going uphill. All McCrea could do was sit there and let the reins hang slack. Hours passed. He looked up at the stars and saw the Big Dipper. The air was cold and he wore nothing warmer than his cotton shirt. He had to clinch his jaws to keep his teeth from chattering, but he refused to let the cold bother him. He had other worries.

"Lordy," McCrea mumbled.

Gradually the sky widened, and now he could see the Little Dipper to the south. Then the realization came to him. "We're getting out of the canyon, old pony. We're coming to the top." He reached down and scratched the horse's neck. "Good boy. If we get to that girl in time, she's going to owe you her life."

He knew he was out of the canyon when he was able to see the sky all around him. A sliver of a moon appeared to the west. He felt exuberant. "We made it, old pony. You made it."

But in his mind's eye he could see a pretty dark-haired young woman being tortured by two bullies, and the terrible urgency came back. "Now we've got to find that cabin."

Chapter Thirteen

A grey pack rat ran down the wall and across the foot of the wooden bunk where Crystal Lee Brown lay. She could barely see it in the lamplight, but she knew what it was. She shuddered, remembering hearing someone say once that when people move out of the mountain cabins the pack rats and mice move in. She had been lying awake all night listening to the mice scurrying around on the wooden floor of the one-room cabin—and to the snores of the men.

The men were asleep. She could tell by their snoring. She slowly sat up. They had left the oil-burning lamp lit. Why, she did not know. But it enabled her to see the burlap window curtain on the far side of the room move slightly in the breeze from outside. There was no glass in the two windows, only tattered feed sacks. They had built a fire in the small cast-iron stove, but it had burned out an hour ago.

Now that the two men were asleep, she had to first retrieve her shoes from under the man by the door, and then she had to slip out the window on the far side of the room.

There was no chance of getting out the door. One man, the ugly one with the scar down his left cheek, was sleeping on a pallet on the floor next to it, and the door opened inward. The other window, the largest one, was out of the question, too. The second man, the broad-shouldered one with the Texas drawl, was sleeping under it. That left the small window across the room. But first she had to get her shoes. She couldn't run far in the mountains barefoot.

At first when they had carried her kicking out of her cabin in Bluebird, she was too terrified to think. They had put her on a horse, tied her hands to the saddle horn and ridden away in the dark, leading the horse that carried her. Crystal Lee Brown was used to riding. Riding had become her favorite recreation since moving to Bluebird. But her long nightdress and robe were hardly the proper garb.

Her dress was pulled above her knees as she sat astraddle the horse, and her bare legs took a beating in the brush.

When daylight came, the two men could not keep their eyes off her bare knees, but they did not touch her. After they had been riding for a few hours, her mind began to take over from the fear, and she tried desperately to find a way to escape. They did not give her a chance.

Even when she begged to be allowed her toilet, the two men watched while she went behind a clump of willows. And when they climbed out of the canyon and got to the cabin in a high valley just under snow-covered Squaw Peak, the fear returned.

Whatever they planned to do, here was where they were going to do it. And sure enough, the scar-faced one told the other man to leave him alone with her for awhile. The other man said something about how "the boss" wanted her unhurt until he got there, but the scar-faced one leered at her and said she was used to it.

She owed the broad-shouldered man something. He had saved her. Whether it was gallantry or fear of the boss, she did not know, but he had stuck to his argument until finally the scar-faced one backed down.

They had not hurt her, but she knew something awful was coming. From their conversation she was able to figure out what was happening. They thought she knew something about the location of Mr. Levi's mine, and they thought someone else knew something about it, too. They had kidnapped "that other feller," and had forced, or were forcing, him to tell what he knew. Then the boss was to join them here at this cabin and find out what she knew. With the information they got from the two of them, they would be able to find the hidden mine.

What was even more terrifying was the fact that she knew nothing. Would they believe her? Or would they torture her some way until she died? At first she had no idea who "that other feller" was until one of the men mentioned "the cowboy." Then she knew.

It was Mr. McCrea, the nice-looking young man with the troubled eyes, the man who had helped them with their work one evening. Yes, he had to be the one. He had found Mr. Levi dying, and there were people in Bluebird who believed the old man had confided in him. Had they killed him? She shivered when she thought about it. Yes, they had killed him. Or they would. They couldn't let him live. Nor her. They both had to die.

She had to escape.

Crystal Lee Brown was thankful for the lamplight.

Holding her skirt above her ankles to keep from tripping over it, she tiptoed to the man beside the door. She could see her deerskin night slippers, the ones Aunt Agnes had given her long ago, between him and the door. But his body was against them.

Stealthily, she bent over the man and, holding her breath, reached for a slipper. The man continued snoring. Slowly, she pushed the slipper out from under him, then picked it up and placed it on the floor behind her.

Her heart stopped when the man suddenly let out a groan and rolled over, facing her. She jerked her hand away and hurried as quietly as she could back to the bunk. There, she stopped and looked back.

The man was breathing heavily again. He had not awakened.

She tiptoed back to him, squatted, reached over him and picked up the other slipper. Then with both slippers in her hand, she made her way quietly to the small window across the room.

The night outside was totally black, but she remembered that the ground sloped slightly upward from there to a spruce and pine forest about two hundred feet to the south. That was where she would go. Maybe she could hide there. Maybe the townsmen would discover her missing and come looking for her and she would be safe. Maybe. But first she would have to get out of the cabin without awakening the two men.

Getting out would be difficult if not impossible. She was not at all certain that she could squeeze through the small window. The other window would be easier, but the broad-shouldered man was sleeping under it.

Moving cautiously, Crystal Lee picked up the only

chair in the room and carried it to the small window. She stood on it, pushed the burlap curtain aside and put her head and shoulders through the window. She squirmed forward and tried to get her hips through but could not. Her clothes wrinkled at the hips. She just could not get through.

Unless . . .

With her eyes on her captors, she undressed. First the wool robe and then the long nightdress. It would be awful, terrible, if the men should awaken and see her this way. Goose bumps stood out on her skin. She had to do it.

She tossed her clothes out the window and put her head through. Then her shoulders. She wriggled and squirmed. Yes, she could get through now. But she had to be careful. Very quiet and careful. Now she was lying with her stomach on the windowsill. She raised her feet from the chair, careful not to accidentally kick the chair. She wriggled until she was hanging head down outside the cabin with her hips inside.

She could touch the ground now. Wriggling, she got her hips outside. Skin was scraped from her thighs as she slid across the windowsill and fell in a heap onto the ground.

She couldn't just lie there. She had to get up and get away, and she had to do it now, without even putting on her clothes. Unmindful of the cold night air, Crystal Lee Brown picked up her clothes and ran.

Rocks hurt her feet, but she ran on anyway, expecting to hear a shout from the cabin and heavy footsteps running after her. Twice, she tripped over rocks and bunch grass and fell. The second time, she fell into a shallow draw, and her face and shoulder were bruised.

For a moment, she lay there, breathing heavily and

listening. There was no noise. The ruckus she had expected did not happen. It was all right now to get dressed. She put the slippers on first, then pulled the nightdress over her head. The warm wool robe came next.

Now she had to get as far away from the cabin as she could. Which way to go? Back toward Bluebird. If anyone was looking for her, maybe she would see them.

With nothing more to guide her than her own sense of direction, Crystal Lee Brown walked and stumbled in the dark, going back the way she believed she had come.

It was hopeless, trying to find the cabin in the dark, and John McCrea finally had to give up and wait for daylight. There was no trail for the horse to follow in the valley, and the night was still darker than the inside of a hip pocket.

He dismounted and loosened the cinches. He took his catch rope from the saddle, tied the end of it to the end of the bridle reins and tied the other end to his belt. Now the horse could graze without getting away and leaving him afoot.

There was nothing to do now but wait for daylight. McCrea sat on the ground and hugged his knees, trying to keep his teeth from chattering in the cold.

"Lordy," he said, shivering.

It was never this cold in the Pecos Valley in New Mexico Territory. Or was it? Well yes, the temperature did get below freezing at times in the coldest part of the winter, but it never snowed, and a man didn't suffer in the cold down there the way he did in the Colorado high country. Or did he?

Well yes, McCrea could remember times when he was numb with cold, standing watch over a bunch of cattle all night, getting out at daybreak in the mornings. Yes, a man could suffer in the cold down south, too. The difference, McCrea decided, was the humidity and the way men dressed. At home he had never worn anything warmer than an unlined denim jacket and unlined leather gloves. In the high country, men wore sheepskin coats, high-crowned Scotch caps that covered the ears, and choppers' mittens with two pairs of wool linings.

It was ironic, McCrea thought, the way some cowmen snort up their sleeves at sheep, yet they wear sheepskin coats during the day and sleep between wool blankets at night. "Lordy," McCrea muttered, he sure could use one of those sheepskin coats right now.

Every ten minutes or so, McCrea had to stand up, stomp his feet and wave his arms to keep from freezing. He would have bet there was ice in the creeks that morning. But maybe not. Maybe it just seemed that cold.

Was the sky getting light in the east? Lordy, he hoped so. Hurry up, daylight.

After she had fallen several times and run into the trees, Crystal Lee Brown decided she would have to wait for daylight. If she wandered too much in the dark, she could become hopelessly lost. Men had become lost in the high country. Lost and died.

Her wool robe kept off most of the chill, but her feet in the thin deerskin slippers were cold. She sat on the ground and folded her legs under her, to where the robe covered her feet. She sat that way for a half hour, until her knees became cramped, and she had to stand and stretch. Was the sky getting lighter in the east? Yes. It would be daylight soon, and she could go on. Go where?

Let's see now, the sun comes up in the east. Well, at this time of year it would be a little to the south, wouldn't it? Yes. And she had had the presence of mind the day before to keep track of the directions they were taking. First it was east on the San Lomah Road, then north. So the thing to do now was to keep the sun on her left and go south. Perhaps if she went far enough south she would come to the San Lomah Road.

But there was a lot of rough country between here and there, a lot of high ridges, dense forests, and deep ravines. A body could know which direction to take in the mountains and still not be able to find a way out because of so much impassable country.

And how far was it to the San Lomah Road? Twenty miles? Thirty? Well, she decided, she would rather be lost in the mountains than be at the mercy of a gang of thugs.

Gradually, the sky lightened, and finally she could make out the trees. She found herself just inside a thick stand of pine and spruce on the edge of the valley. She could see across the valley now to what looked to be the foot of Squaw Peak. Distance was deceiving to the eye, but it looked to be five miles across the valley. It was time to go on.

Crystal stretched her cramped legs slowly, pulled the wool robe tighter around her throat and started walking. She stayed just inside the timber on the edge of the valley and walked in the direction she believed to be south. Deep ravines, steep hills, and rock outcroppings were in her way, but she slid down some, climbed others and kept going. The sun had not appeared yet when she found herself on top of an outcropping of granite where she could see the cabin. She stopped and studied the scene a moment. And then her breath caught in her throat.

The two men came boiling out of the cabin. They looked in all directions, ran to the other side of the cabin and looked some more. They ran to a wire pen and to their horses. Soon they were mounted. They sat their horses and talked for a moment, then split up. One man rode west and the other turned his horse south.

And he was coming right toward her.

The rider was looking in all directions as well as toward Crystal. Twice, he stopped and studied the country. But he kept coming. Crystal slid off the boulders and ran. She stayed inside the woods and skirted the open areas, but when she got to where she could look back, she realized she had made a mistake.

The rider had seen movement and he knew it had to be her. He was coming now on a gallop.

She ran. Holding her skirts off the ground, she ran, tripped and fell, got up and ran. Her breath was whistling in her lungs, and when she looked back she knew it was hopeless. She could not outrun a horse. If only she could find a hiding place, a bunch of boulders, a deep ravine, anything.

And then the horse was right behind her. She ran. The horse hit her knocking her flat. Before she could get up the rider was on the ground, grabbing at her. She broke free and ran, but he caught her and wrestled her to the ground. She screamed. It was the scar-faced man, and he grinned cruelly. He sat astraddle her writhing body, chuckling. She scratched at his eyes, but he grabbed her wrists in one of his big hands and chuckled again.

"You little whore. I'm gonna treat you the way a

whore oughta be treated." He was unbuttoning her robe and pulling it down, and then he was tearing at her nightdress.

"Please. Please don't."

Her pleas were ignored. A hard light came into his eyes as he tore at her dress. She squinched her eyes shut, expecting the worst.

And suddenly, he was no longer there.

One moment he was astraddle her, tearing at her clothes and the next moment he was not there.

Chapter Fourteen

Crystal Lee Brown opened her eyes and saw the scar-faced man being dragged away by the seat of his pants. A rope around his chest had his arms pinned to his sides. He had dropped his gun. The rope was wrapped around a saddle horn on a bay horse. The man on the horse was—no, it couldn't be. Yes. His face was badly bruised and skinned and he looked gaunt, but it was Mr. McCrea.

How could it be? But it was. She had not heard him ride up and neither had the scar-faced man. They had not heard the loop in the lariat sing through the air and settle around the scar-faced man's chest.

Now the cowboy had dismounted and was pointing a pistol at the man.

"One wrong move, mister, and you're dead."

The hoodlum sat on the ground, blinking in disbelief. "Who—where'd you come from?"

Ignoring his question, the cowboy turned to the young woman. "Are you hurt, Miss Brown? Did they hurt you?"

"No," she said uncertainly. "He didn't hurt me. How

did you get here?"

McCrea didn't know how to answer her question in a few words and he said, "I'll tell you about it later. We've got to get this man back to town."

And then the hoodlum was charging the cowboy. With his head down, he grabbed at McCrea's legs while the cowboy was talking to her.

McCrea was staggered by the man's rush. He tripped over a rock and fell heavily with the man on top of him. He grabbed McCrea's gun arm with both hands and tried to wrestle the gun away from him.

Crystal Lee Brown watched, horrified. She had never seen men fighting like this. These men were fighting for their lives. The loser would be killed. She could not allow Mr. McCrea to be killed. What could she do?

She did what women do naturally in such situations: She grabbed at the scar-faced man's hair and pulled and scratched.

The man was big and heavy, and McCrea could not get out from under him. He stabbed at the man's face with his fingers, but that had little effect. He clawed at the man's eyes, but the man ducked his head and continued trying to wrestle the gun out of McCrea's right hand.

Then suddenly the pressure lessened. The man was leaning backward. McCrea managed to turn on his side and free his gun hand. They scrambled up at the same time, but McCrea had the gun and the other was at his mercy.

But the hooligan did something McCrea did not expect. He turned and ran. He ran awkwardly like a man not accustomed to running, but he ran, his jack boots clomping over the hard ground and the rocks. McCrea raised the gun and got the man's broad back in the sights.

"Hold it," he yelled.

The man continued running, stumbling at times but keeping his balance.

"Stop, mister."

The man did not look back. Soon he was down in a shallow draw, and he turned and ran along the bottom of it. McCrea could see only his head and shoulders now, but the man was still an easy target.

Holding the gun out at arm's length with the hammer back, McCrea watched the man climb out of the end of the draw and disappear in the timber. He watched for a long moment after the man had disappeared, then lowered the gun and turned to face the young woman.

"I should have shot him, but I couldn't. I can't shoot a man in the back."

"I understand."

McCrea let the hammer down gently and holstered the gun. He stepped toward the young woman. "Are you sure you're all right?"

"Yes. But there's another man down there somewhere."

"I know. I saw him."

She clutched the robe tightly around her. "There will be more. They said someone was to join them here today."

"It'll take most of the day to get here, and that other man, whoever he is, won't be back for awhile. Last time I saw him he was going west, toward that peak up there."

"What should we do, Mr. McCrea?"

"Maybe we ought to go back to that cabin. I could use some chuck. We'll have to keep an eye out for them."

"What should we do if their cohorts come along?"

"It'll be late in the day before they can get here, and

doubt they'll get here at all. I left word for the sheriff to come up here. He was out of town yesterday, but he must have got my message by now, and he ought to be here with a posse before dark."

"Then you think the hoodlums will find out the sheriff is coming up here and will stay away?"

"That's what I'm hoping. There's two men out there now, but they've only got one gun. I don't think they'll try to sneak up on us in the daylight, and the sheriff should be here before tonight."

"Whatever you say, Mr. McCrea."

McCrea walked over to where the scar-faced man had dropped his six-gun, picked it up and stuck it inside his belt. "Is there anything to eat in that cabin?"

"Yes. They brought some canned goods and flour with them yesterday, and there are blankets."

"If I don't get something to eat pretty soon I'm not going to be much good. And my horse has gone far enough for awhile, and that man's horse can't carry both of us."

"There is another horse in a pen near the cabin. It's the horse that carried me yesterday."

"Oh sure. I forgot about that one. McCrea lifted his hat, ran his fingers through his brown hair and reset his hat. "I'd like to give my old pony a day's rest before we start back to town. Maybe we ought to wait for the sheriff and go back tomorrow."

"Perhaps you are right, Mr. McCrea."

"Can you ride a horse?"

"Oh yes, I can ride."

"Of course." McCrea grinned sheepishly. "You rode up here. Tell you what. I know my horse is gentle, so why don't you ride him and I'll ride that hooligan's horse."

133

"Fine." She went to McCrea's bay gelding and picked up the reins. As before, her dress and robe hiked above her knees when she got into the saddle, but the cowboy seemed to be more embarrassed at that than she was.

He caught the other horse, mounted and led the way toward the cabin in the valley. As they rode, McCrea kept a constant watch out for the other hoodlum and advised Miss Brown to do the same. "Sooner or later they'll come back, and we'll have to deal with them," he said.

They put their horses in a half-acre pen encircled by patched-up hog wire. A long pole stock shelter, enclosed on three sides with the open side facing the pen, stood at one end. The pen, which had once held sheep, had not held livestock for several years, and the grass in it had grown high. A hand-dug ditch carried water through it from a nearby creek. McCrea allowed that his horse could rest and eat his fill there.

"Do you want me to stay outside and watch while you eat?" she asked.

"Tell you what. You eat while I watch, and then I'll eat while you watch."

Inside the cabin, Crystal built a fire in the small cook stove, opened a can of beef hash and mixed some biscuit dough with the flour and baking soda she found. There was no coffeepot, and she boiled coffee in an empty coffee can. When the meal was ready, she set a tin plate, a cup of hot coffee, and a knife and fork on the small wooden table. She placed the tin of hot biscuits, the hash, and a half-full jug of corn syrup beside them and went to the door.

"Breakfast is ready, Mr. McCrea. It's my turn to watch."

"All right. If you see anybody, holler." He went in and

was pleasantly surprised to find the meal laid out and ready. He dug in.

While he ate he looked around the room and was surprised to find it stocked with groceries and blankets. Someone had been using the cabin, and it was not the sheep man and it was not Diamond J. It had to be prospectors. They had discovered the cabin while they were looking for gold. Or looking for Old Levi's hidden mine.

It was probably the latter, McCrea surmised.

The cabin was well built, but the logs were rotting out now. Whoever had built it had left the bark on the logs, and McCrea knew that unskinned logs deteriorated in a few years. Even the skinned ones not soaked in creosote lasted only eight or ten years. As Judson Olesky had once said disgustedly, "The only thing that decomposes in this damn climate is fence posts and building logs."

McCrea devoured most of the food before he noticed that she had not eaten.

Still chewing, he went outside. "You put one over on me, Miss Brown." He grinned. "I thought you had already helped yourself."

"You were so nearly starved that you looked faint."

"To tell the truth, I was feeling kind of weak in the knees." His grin turned into a wide smile. "I hope I left enough."

"If you didn't, I'll prepare some more."

"Those sure are good biscuits. And you make better boiled coffee than any man."

"Thank you, Mr. McCrea. Shall I bring you another cup?"

"Yes, ma'am, if you would please."

Carrying the tin coffee cup and taking a sip now and

then, McCrea walked around the cabin, eyes studying the countryside. He took a circle around the long sheep shed at the end of the pen and started back to the cabin. He saw the rider coming.

The rider was so far away that McCrea could not see his face, and he knew the man could not recognize him either. McCrea hurried back to the one-room cabin, told Crystal Lee Brown to be prepared to run if anything happened to him, then slipped out the door. He circled the cabin and hid behind the sheep shed.

By that time, the rider was close enough that McCrea recognized him as one of the men he had seen in the Bluebird Cafe and again in The Palace Saloon. He was a professional hoodlum, all right. McCrea cocked his .44, waited until the rider dismounted at the gate to the pen, then stepped out from behind the shed.

"Hold it," he barked. "Don't move or I'll blow a hole in you."

The rider stiffened and looked back over his shoulder.

"Don't move." McCrea came up behind him, lifted his six-gun from its holster and dropped it onto the ground. He stepped back. "All right, mister, turn around and keep your hands up."

The man turned slowly. His eyes registered surprise when he recognized McCrea. "But—"

"I'm supposed to be dead, ain't I? Walk over to that cabin and be mighty careful. I'm a killer, you know, and you might be next."

At the cabin, McCrea called for Miss Brown to come out. When she appeared in the doorway, he asked her if this was the other man who had kidnapped her. When she identified him, McCrea muttered, "I ought to shoot you, mister."

"No, don't," she said, coming to stand beside McCrea. "He helped me."

"He did? How?"

"The other man wanted to—harm me and he talked him out of it."

The broad-shouldered man hurriedly agreed with her, talking with a drawl as broad as Texas. "Ah shore did, Miss Brown, and Ah'm shore glad Ah did. Ah've done some things Ah ain't proud of but Ah ain't never took advantage of no woman like tha-yet."

"You're from Texas, aren't you," Miss Brown said.

"Ah shore am, ma-yum, and Ah know that's where you're from too. And Ah don't ca-yer what you done." The man kept glancing from the gun to Miss Brown and back to the gun.

McCrea couldn't help noticing that the young woman's face suddenly went white and her lips trembled. "Is something wrong, Miss?"

"No." She forced herself to talk normally. "No, I—can you let him go? I mean is there some way you can let him go and be certain he won't come back?"

"Well." McCrea hesitated. "I can't just shoot him down, and well, if he helped you, I guess I can let him go."

"Ah swa-yer Ah won't come back," the man said. "Ah'll do anything you say."

"All right. Get your horse and git. Leave your gun."

"Yes sir, Mr. McCrea. Ah know about you, and Ah ain't gonna git in no gunfight with you. Ah'll do whatever you say."

"All right. Git."

The man hurried to his horse, mounted and rode away at a fast trot.

He was about four hundred yards from the cabin when McCrea realized he had made a mistake in letting him go. In fact, he had made two mistakes.

"Lordy," he groaned.

"What is it, Mr. McCrea?"

Pointing toward the canyon he had ridden out of the night before, McCrea said, "See him? That's the man that ran from us. The man on a horse sees him and he's heading that way."

"Oh yes, I see him."

"And that's not all. I thought we were letting two unarmed men go. I was wrong. That man on a horse has a rifle in a boot under his left leg. I didn't see it until now." McCrea shook his head in disbelief. "Everybody else carries a rifle on the off side. That's why I didn't see it."

"What do you think will happen?"

"They'll be back unless the sheriff gets here first. I doubt if they'll be back before it gets dark—it's too hard to sneak up on us out here in the open country—but they need another horse and I'm guessing they'll be back."

"Not only do they need another horse," Miss Brown said, "but they are afraid of their leader. From the way they talked, I gather that they are afraid of what he might do if they fail."

Turning to face her, McCrea asked, "Did they ever mention their leader by name?"

"No. They only referred to him as 'the boss.'"

"Yeah, that's all I heard, too. I'd give a dollar to know who he is."

"What happened to you, Mr. McCrea?"

He told her in general terms, leaving out the painful details.

"I certainly thank you for coming. I owe you my life. I

138

hope I can repay you somehow."

At that, McCrea grinned. "We're even now. You pulled that scar-faced brute off me back there."

"You would not have been in that predicament were it not for me."

"Forget it." McCrea walked to the cabin. "Let's see what else we can find to eat. It's going to take a lot of chuck to get the wrinkles out."

Crystal followed him, but she had to look back over her shoulder at the two men, one on foot and the other on horseback, a half-mile away, far out of pistol range.

She wondered how far a rifle could shoot.

Chapter Fifteen

It was hard to keep his eyes open, but John McCrea had to do it. He had not slept for, how long? Two days and nights? It seemed like a year ago that he had been awakened in his bedroll out on the edge of Bluebird. He was weary almost to the point of collapse, but he had to keep a lookout.

The easiest way to do that, he had decided, was to use the homemade ladder he had found to climb up on the roof of the cabin. He could see in all directions from there. And to make himself a small target, he lay face down on the dirt roof. That made it even more difficult to stay awake.

The dirt roof was soft. Anything would have seemed soft to a man who had not slept in two days and nights. McCrea's eyelids were heavy. The sun was warm on his back. The roof cradled him comfortably.

He awoke with a snort when he heard his name called. "Mr. McCrea. Mr. McCrea. Are you all right?"

"Huh?" He sat up and looked down at Crystal Lee

Brown. "Huh? Guess I dozed off." He shook his head to clear the sleep from his eyes. "I'm a fine guard, ain't I?"

"It's no wonder you slept, Mr. McCrea, after what you've been through. I slept awhile and came out to see how you were doing. I found you asleep, and I let you alone while I kept watch."

"Well," McCrea said, blinking his eyes, "did you see anything?"

"I saw them near the mouth of that canyon once, and when I looked again I couldn't see them."

"How long ago was that?"

"A half hour ago, I think."

McCrea crawled off the steep roof onto the rickety ladder and from there to the ground. He saw that the sun was near the jagged horizon to the west. How long had he slept?

"We might have a problem here, Miss Brown."

"I know."

"You know?"

"Yes. I've been thinking. What if the sheriff doesn't get here? You said you left a message for him. What if he didn't get it? What will we do?"

McCrea grinned without mirth and shook his head sadly. "That's the problem, all right. I left the message with Judson Olesky, but he and the sheriff might not have seen each other."

"Judson Olesky?"

"Yeah, the boss of the Diamond J cowboy crew. I worked for him for awhile, and I met him while I was following your trail yesterday. He told me about this cabin."

"Then there is a chance that the sheriff didn't get your message."

"I'm afraid you're right."

Nobody spoke for a moment, then she asked, "What do you suggest we do?"

Glancing again at the skyline, McCrea noticed that the sun was sinking fast, and it would soon be dark. "If anybody left Bluebird early this morning, they should have been here by now. If the sheriff doesn't show up pretty soon, Miss Brown, we're in trouble."

She nodded to let him know she understood and asked again, "What do you suggest?"

"If the sheriff doesn't show up then one of two things is happening. Those two are waiting for their boss to come along, and if their boss does come along, they'll probably wait 'til dark to come after us. If their boss doesn't come along—and there's a chance he would want to wait until the sheriff was through searching—then they'll wait 'til dark and try to steal the horses."

"And," she added, "try to murder us in our sleep."

Again, he shook his head sadly. "I'm afraid that's right." A crease appeared between the cowboy's eyes and right then he made up his mind. "Here's what we'll have to do, Miss Brown. We can't guard the cabin and the horses at the same time. We'll have to let them have the cabin, while we nighthawk the horses."

He paused to see if she understood. She nodded affirmatively.

"So the thing to do is go in there and fix something to eat before dark. We have to eat. And when it gets dark we'll take what groceries we can put on a horse and some blankets, and we'll have to spend the night outside by the pen."

She was moving toward the cabin by the time he finished talking. She stopped suddenly and looked back. When she spoke again, she spoke calmly, even though McCrea could see her features stiffen with fear. "What about tomorrow, Mr. McCrea? What will we do then?"

McCrea wanted to say something reassuring, but he could think of nothing. He walked to her and stood before her. "We can't go back the way we came. Those two will be there, hiding behind the boulders with a rifle. And they might have help."

Nodding, Crystal said apologetically, "I'm sorry I got you into this, Mr. McCrea."

"Don't be." He spoke almost harshly. "Don't feel sorry for anything at all. We'll survive."

"How?"

"There's another way out of these hills. I heard the Diamond J cowboys talk once about a way over the divide to some other town north of here."

"I've heard that, too, but I also heard that it's a rough route and one that takes several days, perhaps a week."

"Well, we've got groceries and blankets and three horses. We'll make it."

She studied his face for a moment and spoke softly. "You're a very competent man, Mr. McCrea. I believe you."

They waited until after dark to carry the groceries and blankets out of the cabin. They did not want to be seen, and they knew the cabin was being watched. They found an empty burlap bag and filled the bottom of it with tins of dried beef and tins of beans and other vegetables.

McCrea emptied the flour sack out the rear window. "I hate to waste good flour," he said, "but we need the sack, and I don't care to leave them anything anyway." They filled the bottom of the flour sack with more groceries, some dried peaches, two skillets, and a box of wooden matches.

They gathered all five of the blankets they found, and McCrea was disappointed when they had not found a tarpaulin for a ground sheet. "Oh well, I've camped out with a lot less than this," he said.

Clouds had gathered on the western horizon just before sundown, and the sunset had been brilliant as the sinking sun reflected upward against the clouds. And now the clouds had blotted out the stars and the quarter moon, creating a night that was totally black.

They slipped out of the cabin in the dark and groped their way to the sheep pen. There, working by feel, McCrea dragged a half-dozen logs from beside the shed and stacked them before the wire gate. He piled the three saddles on top of them. The logs were dry and half rotten, but they would make it difficult for anyone to open the gate in the dark. They would also provide a small fortress in a gunfight.

She put her blankets down inside the open-sided shed, and he dropped his beside the gate, behind the stack of logs. He sat on a folded blanket and wrapped the other around his shoulders.

She whispered, "Good night, Mr. McCrea. I'm glad it was you who came after me."

"Good night," he whispered and smiled in the dark. What did she mean by that? Did she think him somebody special? She was some woman. Every inch a lady, but no bloomer button and no bellyacher. She had almost escaped by herself, and when she had had to fight, she had fought. Yes sir, she was some woman.

And now, he thought, the smile leaving his face, he had to stay awake. No more sleeping on the job.

It was pleasant sitting there in the dark. He could hear the horses cropping the grass and blowing through their nostrils. A coyote yap-yapped somewhere at the edge of the timber. Another joined in, yipping and yapping excitedly. They sounded like a herd of coyotes, but they were probably only a couple of pups, McCrea surmised. They sounded like hysterical laughter.

Now that he had a warm blanket, he enjoyed listening to the coyotes, the horses, and the other night sounds in the high country. And no rattlesnakes. That was one of the things McCrea liked about the mountains. Snakes couldn't stand the altitude. He remembered times when he had slept on the ground in the New Mexico Territory and had lain awake for hours, wondering if that slight movement he had felt at the foot of his bed, or thought he had felt, was a rattlesnake. It makes a man afraid to move or even to breath, he remembered grimly.

But the only snakes he had seen up here were the harmless little black ones he had seen near the creeks. It was good to know there were no rattlesnakes.

His eyelids were getting heavy again. Lordy. He slapped his face, trying to shock himself into alertness. Lordy, it was hard to stay awake.

McCrea's head dipped. He snorted awake and straightened up. He sat cross-legged until his knees ached, and he had to stand up. He stretched one leg at a time, careful to make no noise, and sat again.

One of the horses was coming up to water. Through the fog in his mind, McCrea could hear the hoofbeats approaching slowly. Hoofbeats? He came awake instantly, nerves taut. They were coming.

Listening, straining his ears, McCrea heard the hoofbeats stop near the gate. Someone whispered, "Where's the goddamn gate?"

He heard someone touch the wire fence, heard someone swear, "Where the hell is it? Goddammit, I can't find my ass with both hands."

McCrea slid the .44 out of the holster, his thumb on the hammer. He knew that when he cocked the hammer back, the sound would be unmistakable, and he knew that if he fired, they would see the flash and return the fire. He worked his way cautiously down behind the pile of logs and saddles, wishing he could make himself smaller. They would shoot in his direction. They would throw a lot of lead, hoping to get in a lucky shot. But they would also know that he was there guarding the horses, and as long as he was alive, they had no chance of stealing a horse.

No use trying to pick out a target. It was too dark for that. McCrea ducked behind his logs, cocked the hammer back and fired a shot at the sky.

The boom of the old .44 split the night air. Almost immediately more shots were fired, and it was as if hell had suddenly opened up. Bullets hit the logs, hit the ground behind McCrea. One bullet knocked a saddle off the pile. Someone was firing as fast as he could work the lever on a rifle.

But McCrea could tell to his satisfaction that only one gun was firing. There were only two men, and that rifle couldn't hold more than a dozen cartridges.

As suddenly as it had started, the shooting stopped. The night was still again. McCrea kept his head down. A man whispered, "Wonder if I got the sonofabitch."

McCrea raised his head and fired another shot at the sky to answer his question.

He heard footsteps, scuffling, a horse snort, hooves stomping the ground, and a man swear. "Goddammit, all that shootin' spooked my horse. I almost lost him."

He heard footsteps and hoofbeats going away toward the cabin. Smart, he thought. You can't shoot a man out of his fort in the dark. He heard her whisper, "Mr. McCrea, are you all right?"

"Yeah, I'm fine. Stay put."

He heard the cabin door open on rusty hinges. Let them have it. They won't get much. And then a thought came to him. Lordy, I didn't look at everything in that cabin. I hope I didn't leave any rifle bullets behind.

A dim light flared up for a moment inside the cabin, and McCrea guessed that one of the men had lighted a match. They wouldn't be so dumb as to light a lamp and sit inside the cabin where they would be easy targets for anyone shooting through the window. No, they had to search the place by lighting matches. And if they are smart, McCrea thought, one of them will stay outside and listen for anyone approaching. In fact, if they are smart, they won't stay in the cabin. They won't take a chance on being trapped in there.

Sure enough, fifteen minutes after they entered the cabin, they left it. McCrea could hear them whispering, and he could hear the footsteps of the men and a horse as they walked away to the east, toward that canyon.

There, they would wait until daylight and then decide whether to keep trying to kill him and the girl or quit the country. Their decision would depend upon who, if anyone, came up the canyon trail. If it was the sheriff, they would make themselves hard to find. If it was their boss, McCrea and the girl were a long way from being out of danger.

One thing was certain: McCrea and Miss Brown had to leave. They could not just wait around to see what happened. If the boss joined the two thugs, McCrea wanted to be a long way away. And there was only one way to go: over the divide just to the north of that snow-covered peak. He had heard the Diamond J cowboys talk about that trail. It was passable, but barely, for a man on a horse. The only trails up in that part of the country were game trails and the remains of an old Ute Indian hunting trail. How far? McCrea had heard no estimate of the distance, but he had heard that it took four or five long days to get down to a town called Mary's Lake.

It could be not too bad a trip, and it could be impossible. McCrea looked at the sky. Still cloudy. It could snow anytime now in the high country, and two or three inches of snow would cover the ground and make it impossible to follow a dim trail.

"Lordy," McCrea whispered. He had heard stories of men being lost in the mountains and freezing to death. A man weak from hunger could freeze easily. A woman? "Lordy."

Was there any other way? None that McCrea could think of. He worried it over in his mind, and just before daybreak he decided that the only way out of their predicament was to head for the north side of Squaw Mountain. Once across the valley and into the higher hills they could look back, and maybe, if they were lucky, they could see if anyone was following them. If there was no one, maybe it would be safe to return and go back to Bluebird via the canyon trail. Maybe.

The sky was getting lighter on the eastern horizon. It was time to move. McCrea found the girl sitting up in her blankets. It was still too dark to see her face. When she heard his footsteps, she stood up, still wearing the nightdress and woolen robe.

"It's me, Miss Brown. We have to move."

"I was thinking the same thing, Mr. McCrea. We don't know who will arrive here by evening, do we?"

"No, I'm afraid we don't. We have to get away from here just in case it's the wrong people."

"You're right. Which way do you think we should go?"

"Over the divide. Or at least in that direction. If no one follows us, we won't have to go all the way."

"I see. Then if we are not followed, you think it will be safe to go back the way we came?"

"That's what I'm hoping. There's nothing else to do."

"There is no other way back to Bluebird?"

"Not that I know of. We could spend days looking for a way and not find one."

No one spoke for a moment, then she said, "What can I do to help?"

"As soon as we can see let's catch and saddle the horses and be on our way. We can't wait for breakfast."

When the early light came, McCrea caught and saddled two of the horses, and she caught and saddled the other.

"This is the horse I rode up here," she said. "He's sound and gentle."

McCrea shifted groceries from the gunnysack to the flour sack until they weighed about the same, then tied the tops together and hung them across the saddle of the scar-faced man's horse. He piled the blankets on top of the saddle and took the rear cinch off the saddle. With that and his catch rope he fashioned a lash cinch to hold the whole load down tight. They were ready to go.

Crystal Lee Brown climbed into her saddle, and McCrea started to mount up too. But wait. Something had to be done about the way her bare legs were exposed above the knees.

"I saw some old overalls in the cabin," he said. "Anything would be better than what you're wearing."

"You're right." She dismounted. "I'll be right back." She was gone only a few minutes, and when she returned, she was wearing the top half of her nightgown and robe and a ragged pair of men's denim overalls. The overalls were at least three sizes too large, and she had to hold them together with one hand. "They'll be all right as soon as I'm on horseback."

Grinning at the ridiculous way she looked, McCrea pulled a pigging string from the rear rigging rings of his saddle. It was a short rope he habitually carried with which to tie down cattle. "This is better than no belt at all."

Matching his smile, Crystal Lee Brown wrapped the rope around her waist and tied the ends.

By sunup they were five miles from the cabin, and McCrea stopped on the other side of a small rise, dismounted and walked back to where he could see their back trail. He saw no sign of life.

"They're not after us yet," he said, "but it's early. If they wait for reinforcements, they won't get on our trail 'til mid-afternoon or later."

She looked up toward the snow-covered peak. "By that time we ought to be up there in the trees again."

"Yeah. Maybe we'll know more about our future by sundown."

Chapter Sixteen

At mid-morning they stopped by the side of a creek meandering its way across the valley. McCrea unloaded the horse they were using as a pack animal, and together they gathered some wood and built a small fire.

"They'll see the smoke, but they no doubt know where we are anyway. I'd bet anything they watched us leave and saw which way we went."

"No doubt about that," she said.

While she mixed some pancake batter and fried bacon, he walked back to where he could again see across the valley. There was still no pursuit. When she called he went back to the fire and ate his fill. The boiled coffee was especially good.

"Where did you learn to cook like that?" he asked conversationally.

"Oh I—" And then she realized that she had started to tell him about her background. Face flushed, she stammered, "I, uh, just picked it up here and there."

He stared at her a moment, wonderingly, then loaded

the pack horse. Was she running from her past, too? Naw, couldn't be. Yet, it sure didn't take much to make her blush. Blush? Sometimes she turned plumb white when someone started to mention her past. He sneaked a glance at her as they rode on. She had her lips clamped shut, looking straight ahead.

It was afternoon and the sun had broken out of the clouds when they rode into the tall spruce and pine and started uphill. They rode through the timber, dodging tree limbs, and on up to the top of a low ridge. Ahead was a series of ridges, each one higher and each covered with coniferous trees. At the head of the highest ridge sat Squaw Mountain. They rode along the top of the ridge, looking for a place where they could see over the trees below them and out onto the valley. When they came to such a spot, they stopped, sat their horses and studied the landscape.

The cabin was barely visible, and—McCrea felt his pulse quicken—there were men and horses around the cabin.

"Do you see them?" he asked.

"Vaguely," she answered.

They sat their horses, straining their eyes. McCrea was accustomed to looking long distances for cattle, and he counted four men. Only three horses.

"How many do you see?" he asked.

"I think there are four or five or, no, I guess there are only four." She turned to him. "What do you think?"

He hated to tell her what he thought. At first he hoped he was mistaken, but when he saw the sun glint for the second time off one man's belt, and the awkward way the man walked, he knew.

"One of them is one of the two men I got away from. He walks with a limp and he wears a Mexican concha belt."

"Oh yes, I've seen him in the cafe. I think he has suffered a crippling disease. He couldn't be part of a posse, could he?"

"Not likely."

She tried to swallow her fear as she said, "That means that instead of Sheriff Harvey joining the two hoodlums, they were joined by more of their kind."

"I'm afraid so, Miss Brown. Now they've got some help and more guns and horses."

He could see the fear in her eyes when she faced him, but he could also see the struggle within her as she fought down the fear. "And you think they will follow us and try to kill us?"

McCrea couldn't look her in the eye. He looked down at his saddle and shook his head sadly. "I'm afraid so, Miss Brown."

Shortly before dark they came to a small waterfall where a creek tumbled down a five-foot rocky embankment, and Crystal Lee said it would be a good place to camp. McCrea disagreed.

"It's a good place to eat a cold meal and drink all the water we can hold, but I'd like to get away from the creek before we settle in for the night. If anybody comes looking for us, they'll probably follow the creek."

"You're right, Mr. McCrea."

They ate from the cans while the horses grazed, and went on. They were in a land of huge boulders again, and McCrea watched for the right spot. Just before dark he found what he was looking for: an acre of lush grass surrounded on three sides by a natural barrier of boulders. He unsaddled two of the horses and used his saddle horse and catch rope to drag two fallen trees up to the only opening. He turned all three horses inside the enclosure and used the dead trees to bottle them up.

He carried the blankets to a grassy spot in the middle of a small park, thinking that it would be a good place to spend the night. "We're lucky to find a spot like this," he said. "Tomorrow night I might have to use that gunnysack to make some hobbles for the horses."

She chuckled without humor and said glumly, "Yes, we're very lucky aren't we." Then she quickly apologized. "I'm sorry. I didn't mean to be sarcastic. You're absolutely right, we are lucky. I mean, I'm lucky. I'm very lucky you came to help me."

Grinning in the darkness, he said, "We could be in worse shape. As it is, we've got horses, chuck, and blankets. We're going to be a lot more comfortable than those guys behind us."

She smiled, but he could tell it was a forced smile. "We are going to survive, aren't we Mr. McCrea?"

"Yeah, we're going to survive."

She spread her blankets and crawled between them, fully dressed. He sat in the dark, silent, smoking, but keeping his hand over the cigarette to prevent any light from escaping.

"Mr. McCrea."

"Uh-huh."

"Could I—could I call you by your first name? Johnny."

He looked her way but could see only a vague outline of her in the dark. "Sure. That is, if I can call you by your first name."

"Call me Crystal Lee. Or just Crystal."

"All right."

"It just seems that—after all, we shouldn't have to be so formal anymore."

"You're right, Miss Brown. Excuse me, Crystal."

"I'm glad the sky cleared. I can see the stars."

"Uh-huh."

"Johnny?"

"Yeah."

"Do you think we're safe tonight?"

"Yeah. They aren't likely to stumble around in these rocks and trees in the dark looking for us."

"Johnny, I, uh, I heard that you came from the New Mexico Territory. Is that right?"

He could see by her vague shape that she had turned on her side and was resting her head on her arm. "That's right."

"I heard, too, that you, uh—"

"Yeah, I know. And yeah, that's true too." Strangely, he was not irritated at her probing. For the first time, when someone had probed into his background, he did not feel irritated.

"All I can say is that you have been a complete gentleman, and anything that happened in your past had to have been something that you could not have avoided."

He didn't reply, but for a moment he considered telling her all about his past. It would be good to talk to someone about it, and he was sure she would understand. A man needed someone to talk to. But not now. Maybe sometime, but not now. He lay back and pulled the blankets over him, hoping she would say no more.

All she said was, "Good night, Johnny."

Johnny McCrea was surprised when he woke up at dawn and found snow on his blankets. He stood up fully dressed except for his boots. He was glad he had put his boots under the blankets with him. It was the first snow of the season, and it barely covered the ground. The sky was clear. McCrea guessed that the snow would melt away soon after the sun came up. The girl was still asleep. He walked quietly when he went to check on the horses, and he tried to be quiet when he built a fire and started frying bacon and boiling coffee. It was the sound of bacon frying that woke her.

Crystal Lee Brown sat up with a start and looked around wildly for a moment before she remembered where she was. She smiled when she saw McCrea squatting beside the fire. Stretching, she stood up in her baggy denim overalls and stepped into her slippers. The deerskin slippers were cold and she grimaced. McCrea grinned.

"You sleep out very much, you learn to take your clothes to bed with you."

She shivered and her smile returned. "I'm learning, Mr. McCrea. Johnny." She came to the fire and held her hands over the flames. "Ooh, that feels wonderful. The bacon and coffee smell wonderful. Where did the snow come from? The stars were out when I went to sleep last night."

"I've heard people say the weather is unpredictable in the high country, especially this time of the year."

"Do you think the smoke will attract our, uh, pursuers?"

"It might, but we have to eat."

She excused herself and went behind a pile of boulders. When she returned they ate, saddled their horses and loaded the packhorse. With little conversation, they rode back to the creek where they both washed their faces in icy cold water. They mounted again and rode on, climbing steadily.

At the top of the next ridge, they stopped and looked over the tops of the trees below them. By that time the sun was up and the temperature was warming up. McCrea squinted out across the terrain below them and saw what he feared he would see.

"Smoke," he said.

"Where? Oh, I see it. It's their camp fire, isn't it?"

"Has to be."

"Then we definitely are being pursued."

"No doubt about it."

"Can we stay ahead of them, Johnny?"

"We can travel as fast as they can. But we can't push these horses too hard. We've got a long way to go, and all this uphill travel is hard on horses."

"And you're afraid they might not be so considerate of their horses."

"Depends on how bad they want to catch us."

They turned their horses and went on, down one small hill and up another, steeper one, always keeping the right side of Squaw Peak as their goal. As yet, they had found no trail and were picking their way around the steepest hills and through the trees. They had to stop periodically, study the terrain and try to find the easiest route.

"There's supposed to be an old Ute Indian trail through here somewhere," McCrea said. "I'd like to find it."

They broke out of the timber and found themselves facing another high, steep ridge. They turned and rode along the bottom of it, following a small stream, looking for a place to climb it. Suddenly, McCrea reined up.

"Look." He pointed to a spot about a hundred yards uphill from them.

She rode up beside him. "Do you see something?"

"Yeah, but I don't know what. Right up there. See?"

"Oh yes. It's a pile of dirt and rocks. What in the world . . ."

Reining his horse uphill, McCrea said, "Whatever it is, it's man-made."

The horses were blowing hard when they got to it. "A hole in the ground," McCrea said.

"And look, Johnny. A ladder sticking out of it, a homemade ladder."

The two of them stared at the hole. It was about fifteen feet deep and no more than eight feet across. The ladder was made from sections of tree trunks. A rusty bucket with a frayed rope attached lay on the ground beside the dirt and rock that had been piled beside the hole.

"A prospector's hole," McCrea said. "I've heard about them. It was dug by someone looking for a vein of gold. Whoever dug it saw something around here that made him think he might strike a vein."

She spoke softly, almost reverently. "I wonder if it was Mr. Levi."

"I'll bet it was either him or his partner." McCrea turned in his saddle and studied the country behind them. He saw no one. "Well, whoever dug it didn't find anything here. I wonder what he saw that made him think he might."

"It must have been terribly hard work, and all for

nothing. Just think, Johnny, someone had to dig that hole with a pick and shovel and carry the dirt up the ladder in a bucket."

McCrea shook his head. "Prospecting is darn hard work. Anybody that gets rich that way deserves it."

"Poor Mr. Levi."

"Yeah." The memory of the dying man caused McCrea's jaw muscles to tighten. "We have to go on, Crystal."

The creek went underground a mile further on, and they found themselves walled in on three sides. They could either go back the way they had come or climb. They chose to climb. Instead of going straight up the hill, they traversed it, making a half-dozen switchbacks. Four times before they got to the top they stopped and allowed the horses to blow. Each time, McCrea scanned the country behind them carefully. Still no one. But he knew men were back there somewhere with rifles, and they could probably follow tracks. It was impossible not to leave tracks of some kind.

When they got to the top of that hill, they found themselves near the foot of Squaw Mountain, and McCrea stopped to look up at it. "It snowed a lot more up there then it did down where we were," he stated.

The breeze that swept across the hill was a chilly one, and she shivered. "I'll bet the snow gets terribly deep up here in the winter."

McCrea's eyes narrowed and he pointed again, this time to the top of the peak. "Look. At first I thought that was a cloud up there, but now I think it's blowing snow."

Crystal's eyes followed where he pointed. "It does look like a small cloud except that it's moving without going anywhere."

"The wind must be blowing fierce up there. And there must be a lot of snow up there, too."

She shivered again. "I'm glad we're down here."

A frown appeared between McCrea's eyes. "We've got to get on over the divide, Crystal. The weather could change anytime. I sure would hate to be snowed in up here."

It was afternoon when they stopped to eat a cold lunch. They picked a spot where the horses could graze out of sight of the country behind them, but where McCrea could crawl to the edge of a cliff and study their back trail.

"Do you see anyone?" she asked.

"No. I think we're almost a day ahead of them."

"Is it possible that they could give up and go back?"

"It's possible, but we can't count on it."

"No, I guess not. How far do you think it is to the top of wherever we're going?"

"Another day, probably. Depends on how rough the country is. We have to keep going to the right of that mountain. I sure would like to find that Indian trail."

Chapter Seventeen

They cinched up and mounted, and within an hour found themselves above timberline. The few trees they saw here were stunted and dead, standing like sentinels. Huge boulders had been piled everywhere by an earth upheaval and moving ice and water a million years earlier. A bald eagle soared above them, its white head shining in the sunlight. A cold wind, no longer hampered by tall timber, whipped around them and sang in their ears. Once, when they rounded a pile of boulders, they saw a small herd of mountain goats clambering around on the rocks, feeding on the tundra and alpine grasses.

Now they were circling the peak, trying to find a way to go to the north side of it. The north side looked to be almost smooth with pure white snow. It rose steeply.

This time it was Crystal Lee who pointed and said, "Johnny, look."

McCrea looked where she pointed. "Well, I'll be damned. Darned."

What they saw was a flat rocky meadow below them, and what puzzled them was the presence of tops of perhaps thirty pine trees lying on the meadow at the foot of a high tree-studded hill. Above the hill was the north face of Squaw Mountain. And what they saw on the side of the hill caused McCrea to suck in his breath in wonderment.

"Lordy."

"Are you thinking the same thing I am?" she asked, speaking softly.

"There's only one explanation. The snow had to have been so deep last winter it covered all but the tops of those trees. Look. You can see where the tops of the tall trees were sheared off."

Turning to face him, Crystal Lee Brown whispered, "Avalanche."

"Yeah." He spoke barely above a whisper himself, feeling somewhat awestruck. "You can see where it sheared off the tops of the trees and carried them down to that clearing."

"My goodness." She was still whispering, as if she feared she might disturb the gods. "It's awesome."

They sat their horses, spellbound at the sight of what nature could do. "It makes me feel terribly small and insignificant, Johnny."

"It can sure make a feller feel small, all right. As far as that mountain is concerned, we're nothing but two little specks."

She shivered. "It's fascinating, but it's scary, too. I suddenly feel as if—as if we are all alone in the universe, Johnny."

Her words reminded him that they were not alone. They were being hunted. He urged his mount on and she followed.

The hill was too steep there, and they had to turn

downhill, back into the timber, trying to keep in a northerly direction. They crossed the small meadow and rode into the timber again. McCrea kept looking for a trail, any kind of a trail.

Camp that night was a cold one. Not wanting to give away their position, McCrea advised against a fire. They opened cans of dried beef and fruit and ate from the cans. McCrea had to empty the burlap sack and cut it into strips for hobbles. He kept his saddle horse on a picket made from his catch rope. That way, he knew he would have at least one horse come morning, and the horse was used to being picketed. It would eat the grass and rest.

It was essential that the horses eat and rest, he told Miss Brown. "Right now, their health is just as important as ours. Maybe more important." She spread her blankets first, and he carried his a respectful distance away.

Crystal Lee Brown was bone weary. She was used to riding, but not all day and not all up and down hills. Riding in the mountains put a strain on muscles that were not used for riding on the flatlands. And she was worried. Though she tried not to show it, she was worried and scared. Would they get over the divide without mishap? It was so easy to get hurt. A horse could fall, injuring the rider. A winter storm could arrive anytime. Those men could catch up and shoot them from ambush. They could shoot Johnny first. With him shot, she would be helpless. They would kill her, too, but not until they had their pleasure with her.

In spite of her weariness, Crystal Lee Brown lay awake. She turned her head and looked over at the cowboy, covered up to his chin with a blanket, his hat over his face. Why had he come to her rescue? Was it merely frontier gallantry? Would other men have done as much? Because of her, he was in a dangerous predicament. If they survived, could she make it up to him? She owed him her life.

"Johnny?"

"Umph."

"I just wanted to say—I just wanted to say thank you."

He lifted his hat two inches above his face and looked her way.

"That's all I wanted to say. Just thank you."

McCrea lay awake, too. But for the moment he had forgotten about the danger that he and the young woman faced. For a moment he was inflicted with a fever, the fever that had made a few men rich and more men bitter, that had caused murder, robbery, and legal thievery. It was gold fever.

Raising up on one elbow, he looked over at the young woman. "Miss Brown? Crystal?"

She turned on her side. "Yes?"

"Did—did Old Levi say anything at all to you about his mine? Anything at all?"

"No, Johnny. Why do you ask?"

"I was thinking. I have a feeling. Kind of a spooky feeling, but kind of exciting, too. We could be somewhere near that mine."

"What makes you think so, Johnny?"

"The snowslide. Avalanche. I'd forgotten something he did until I saw that. Tell me something. Did Old Levi like sugar in his coffee?"

"Yes he did. He used two spoonfuls."

"Well, when I found him, he tried to talk and couldn't, but he reached to an open bag of sugar and turned it over. I'd forgotten about that. And he pointed at the spilled sugar."

Sitting up, Crystal Lee Brown tried to see McCrea's face in the dark. "So what you're thinking is that he tried to tell you about an avalanche?"

"He must have been trying to tell me something."

They were both wide awake. "Come to think of it, Johnny—"

"What?"

"He did say something once. I thought nothing of it at the time, but now—"

A tinge of excitement crept into McCrea's voice. "What did he say?"

"Well, one time when he was drinking coffee and I tried to be sociable, he sort of winked and accused me of trying to find out where his mine was. But he was good-natured about it as if he didn't mind. I told him I was no miner and wouldn't know what to do with his mine if I found it. And he winked again and smiled and said that if I ever looked for it to—let me try to remember his exact words—'Look out for the walking snow.' Yes, that is exactly what he said."

"He had to have been talking about a snowslide."

"Yes, Johnny, he had to have been talking about a snowslide." After a moment of silence, she asked, "What would you do if we found it?"

"I don't know. I'm like you. I wouldn't know what to do with a gold mine. I wouldn't know gold if it bit me."

Gazing at the sky, McCrea's mind slowly came back to their predicament. "Well, we've got other things to think about. Good night, Crystal."

They were on their way again by sunup. The horses were leg weary, but their steel-shod feet were holding up. Converstaion was light. McCrea was desperate now in his search for a trail. There was only one way over the divide, and it had taken the Indians years to find it. There had to be some semblance of a trail. There had to be something.

Alternately, they climbed above timberline and dipped back into the timber, searching for the easy route. They were riding on the backbone of a long ridge when McCrea stopped at a point where he could see the country behind them. He studied the country carefully. Still no sign of their pursuers. He jerked his head back in the young woman's direction when he heard her sudden intake of breath.

"Johnny. Johnny, look."

He looked.

"Is that a cabin or am I seeing things?"

McCrea squinted in the noonday sunlight. "It sure looks like a cabin. But it's setting kind of strange."

They were looking across a narrow valley to the top of another ridge, and sure enough, a small cabin could barely be seen near a rocky outcropping.

"It's tilted," she exclaimed.

"It sure is."

"I wonder why?"

"I don't know. Do you see any signs of life?"

Using her hand, she shielded her eyes from the sun. "No. Do you?"

"No."

"Shall we go see if there is anyone?"

"Well, it's near where we want to go anyway. Yeah,

let's get over there."

Their horses half walked and half slid down the side of the ridge and made their way to the valley. There, they reined up suddenly again and looked down at the weathered, scattered bones of two large animals. Bits of leather and hardware from halters were scattered near the bones.

"Were they horses?" she asked.

"Mules."

"How can you tell?"

"By their feet. Mules have narrower feet."

"What do you suppose killed them?"

McCrea dismounted and walked around the bones, studying them. "I don't know. Coyotes have got the remains pretty well scattered. There's no way of knowing."

"Strange."

It was another hard climb to the top of the ridge where the cabin sat, what was left of it. When they got to it they found that the east end had been bashed in as if kicked by a giant boot. Without dismounting they rode around the cabin and found the foundation. It was made of rock and was about fifteen feet uphill from the cabin.

"What do you suppose happened, Johnny?"

"I can make a guess."

"What?"

"Snowslide. Avalanche."

Her eyes widened. "Yes. That would explain it, wouldn't it?"

"Yeah. I wonder if—"

"What, Johnny?"

"I wonder if anyone was killed. Those two mules had

to have been picketed down there, and they had to have been covered up by a snowslide, the same snowslide that knocked this cabin off its foundation and shoved it over here."

"Oh my."

McCrea urged his horse on and rode around the cabin, looking in without dismounting. The cabin had only one room and had been made of available materials: logs and mud. The only manufactured furnishing was a thin steel stove with two cooking lids on top. Two chairs, a table, and two bunks were made of sections of small trees with the bark peeled off.

Finally, McCrea dismounted and handed the reins to Miss Brown. "I'm going in and take a closer look."

"Be careful, Johnny. It doesn't look too steady."

"It sure took a beating, all right." Stepping carefully, he entered through the open end. He squatted and looked under the bunks. He went to the stove, opened it and saw nothing but the remains of a wood fire. A tattered sheepskin coat hung on a nail on one wall, and that was all McCrea found. No cooking utensils, no nothing.

When he came out he was even more puzzled than when he went in. "It's mighty queer. Those mules would make a feller think that somebody was living here when the snow hit. I guess whoever it was wasn't at home at the time."

"Could he have been out prospecting or hunting and have come back later to get his belongings?"

"That's one possible explanation."

"What do you think we should do?"

"Go on. There's nobody here, that's for sure, and the way this cabin is setting, I don't think I want to use it for a shelter."

"It will soon be dark, Johnny."

"Yeah, but if those men are any good at tracking they'll follow us here, and I don't want to be around when they get here."

"You're right. We should get as far away as we can before dark."

He mounted and rode on, leading the packhorse heading for a notch he had seen in a ridge just to the north of Squaw Mountain.

McCrea was so busy studying the higher elevations looking for a route, that he would not have seen the grave if she hadn't let out another sudden exclamation.

It was a human's grave, just the right length and width. Someone had buried a human body there and covered it with dirt and rocks. A handmade wooden cross was stuck in the ground at one end. Again, McCrea dismounted squatted and squinted at the cross. There was no name. He straightened up, pushed his hat back and scratched his jaw.

When he looked up at Crystal Lee Brown, he had a crooked grin on his face. "Know what, Miss Brown Crystal?"

"What?"

"I think I've got it figured out." He looked down at the grave, still scratching his jaw. "Let's camp here."

"What about our pursuers?"

"They won't get here for another day. And I'm just busting out with curiosity."

"What are you thinking?"

Without answering, McCrea busied himself with hobbling the horses and making camp. "Just in case the aren't the trackers they ought to be we won't build a fire. We don't want to make it easy for them."

Again, they ate from tin cans and drank from a small stream of snow runoff near the cabin. When he had studied the higher elevations, McCrea had seen snow not far uphill from them, and it was melting and running downhill.

Miss Brown was puzzled at the way McCrea was acting. He seemed to be happy about something, but when she questioned him, all he would say was he had a hunch but wasn't sure.

Finally, when they had eaten the contents of three cans, she faced him. "Will you please tell me what's on your mind?"

He was rolling a cigaret. He paused, shot a glance her way, then lit the cigaret with a wooden match. "All right." He sat on the ground. She sat facing him. "The way I heard it, Old Levi came up this way with a partner about a year ago. No, it was more than a year ago, it was in the summer."

"Yes, that's what I heard, too."

"But sometime last winter he went back to Bluebird half frozen and alone, but with his pockets full of gold dust and nuggets." McCrea's voice was taking on a note of excitement.

"Yes?" Excitement was catching hold of her, too.

Their eyes met and held when he spoke again. "I think Old Levi's partner is buried over there. I think we've found Old Levi's camp."

She spoke breathlessly. "Yes. It adds up. It would explain why he came back alone. But," she added, a frown appearing on her face, "why was he so mysterious about what happened to his partner?" And then she answered her own question, "Because," she spoke slowly, considering her words, "he didn't want anybody coming up here to investigate. He didn't want anybody around here." She paused, and McCrea nodded in agreement. "Because his hidden gold mine is around here somewhere."

Chapter Eighteen

It was frightening the way the human mind worked, Crystal Lee Brown mused as she lay in her blankets. The human animal was a greedy animal. Just the small possibility of finding wealth turned men into carnivorous animals of the worst kind. Just the small chance of finding gold caused men to sell their property, leave their homes, travel thousands of miles and endure all kinds of hardships. It was a disease that invaded men's minds. But it was an exciting disease.

She had seen their faces when just the mere mention of someone's finding gold turned them into children. She had seen them eat breakfast hastily, gobble their food and hurry back to the gold field, thinking that if they worked fast enough they would be the next to strike it rich.

And now, as she lay in her blankets on the rocky ground high in the mountains, Crystal Lee Brown wondered if she were any different. She had to admit that the idea of finding a lost gold mine, a very rich one, was exciting. Were it not for the danger surrounding her and John McCrea, this would be an exciting adventure.

But there was that danger.

Sometime during the night, the sky clouded over and dumped more snow on the high country of southern Colorado, and it settled a question in John McCrea's mind.

When he kicked snow off his blankets the next morning, looked up, saw an overcast sky, more snow falling and Squaw Mountain out of sight up in the clouds, he knew what he had to do.

The young woman awoke as soon as he did and let out a groan when she saw the snow. "What will we do, Johnny?"

"It's decision time, Miss Brown. Crystal." McCrea said no more until he saw to the horses. Fortunately, the snow was only two inches deep, and the mountain grass was a foot high. The horses were doing all right.

But McCrea was looking at the high ridge above them when he went back to where Crystal Lee Brown was stamping her feet and waving her arms to get warm.

"Can we have a fire?"

"No. This snow will make it hard for those hooligans to track us, and I don't want to send them a smoke signal. I saw a sheepskin coat in the cabin. I'll fetch it." He went after the coat, and while he was in the cabin, he looked under the bunks again and everywhere a prospector might have hidden something. There was nothing.

She was sitting on a rock with a blanket wrapped around her shoulders when he returned. She put on the coat, and he wrapped a blanket around himself and squatted on his heels before her.

"Here's what we're facing, Miss Brown. This snow is good and bad." He paused long enough to glance again at the high ridge above them. "I can see that it snowed more up there than it did here, and I'm not at all sure we can get over the divide now. The only thing we can do is go back the way we came."

Nodding in agreement, she said, "And hope we can get down before more snow comes."

"Yeah, but the snow is good for us, too. They can't track us now." John McCrea took the tobacco sack out of his pocket, discovered he had only a pinch of tobacco left, and put it back in his pocket for later. "And this snow might turn them around, too. There's something else I'd like to ask you about, Miss Brown. Crystal. What do you think about, uh, maybe—"

She finished the thought for him. "Looking for the lost mine?"

He was relieved that she had put his thoughts into words, and he grinned a small crooked grin. Then he frowned again. "But we'd be taking a chance. The sooner we get down from here the better. I'm not saying it's a smart thing to do."

"It's an opportunity that comes once in a lifetime," she put in. But her thoughts were as clouded as the sky. What John McCrea said was true: The quicker they got to a lower elevation the less danger of being snowed in. He would leave immediately if she asked him to. But he would look back and wonder for the rest of his life if he had passed up an opportunity to strike it rich. She couldn't ask him to do that. And she couldn't leave the decision up to him either, because he would blame himself for the rest of his life if they failed and she suffered unnecessarily. That is, if they survived. She saw the troubled expression on his face, saw him repeatedly studying the sky, weighing their chances. Funny that she should notice it now when she had not noticed it before, but he had several day's growth of beard. The bruises and contusions were healing nicely, though. She remembered that he had a pleasant face under the beard.

"Let's do it, Johnny."

Using his pocketknife, McCrea cut two square pieces from one of the blankets and fashioned a pair of socks for her to wear inside the thin deerskin slippers. They ate from tin cans, looked again at the horses and went hunting for a gold mine.

McCrea grinned crookedly. "It's got to be one of two places. Uphill or downhill. I'm betting it's uphill."

"What if it is placer mining?" she asked, smiling with him.

"You mean panning in a creek or something like that?"

"Yes. I'm no miner but I've heard miners talk."

"All right. There's plenty of water around here."

They left the horses to graze while they searched on foot. The largest stream ran only twenty feet from the remains of the cabin, and McCrea followed it uphill until he saw that it came from a glacier in a crevasse above them. Thin sheets of ice covered the edges of the creek, but running water had kept the stream from freezing solid.

McCrea turned and followed it downhill to where it gurgled happily across the narrow valley, passed the remains of the two mules and went on from there.

"They wouldn't have built their cabin too far away," he said when he got back to where Crystal Lee Brown waited for him. "Let's look for another creek, and keep your eyes open for a cave or a hole in the ground."

They walked, he going in one direction and she in another. Snow runoff was picking up volume now, and McCrea wondered if perhaps the sun was shining above the clouds up there on top of Squaw Mountain, melting the snow. He noticed with some satisfaction that the clouds were moving.

He followed two more streams even though he knew they were just temporary ones made of melting snow, and he turned back to where he had last seen the young woman. He was standing near the cabin wondering where she had gone when he heard her calling to him.

Her voice was coming from thick timber to the west of the cabin, and he went in that direction. He had to call to her and get her answer before he found her. She was standing beside a stream that had to be a permanent one because it had worn its way down to a gravel bed. McCrea walked up beside her and at first didn't see what had attracted her attention. Then he said, "Well I'll be damned. Darned."

"It just appears," she said. "It's coming out of that hill, right out of the side of that hill."

"It's a natural spring. Wonder where it goes?"

They turned downhill and hadn't walked fifty feet before they heard splashing water and knew there was a small waterfall ahead. Sure enough, they came to a clearing an acre wide and saw the creek pouring down a two-foot drop from a rocky ledge into the clearing. There, just beyond the drop, they saw the man-made trough.

Half running, excitement building within them, they got to the wooden trough, stopped and stared.

"What is it, Johnny?"

"I think it's a sluice box."

"I've heard of such things. They say it's faster than panning."

"Yep. See the riffles. Man-made. And look, someone dug gravel out of the creek just below the waterfall and shoveled it into the box."

"The shovel's still there. And there's gravel in the box. Some gravel gets in without shoveling."

McCrea went over and picked up the shovel that was leaning against a boulder, scooped up a shovel of sand and gravel and dumped it into the box.

The force of the water running down the length of the trough washed the sand out the other end. Then McCrea noticed the small basin near the end where the heaviest gravel had gathered. He reached into the cold water and brought a handful of gravel out of the basin. Miss Brown came up and they both stared at what McCrea held in his hand.

"If it's gold it doesn't look like it," she said.

"It can't all be gold," he said, picking out the obvious sandstones. Soon he realized that he held nothing but sandstone. "Well," he said, puzzled, "that's the way it's supposed to work. The water washes the worthless stuff out the other end, and the gold is supposed to settle in this basin."

"Sure, Johnny, but you don't expect to find a nugget in every shovelful of sand, do you?"

He grinned at her. "No, I guess that'd be asking too much." He reached into the basin again and pulled out another handful of gravel. Again, he began picking out the obviously worthless stones.

"There," she said. "Maybe that's one."

He picked out the multicolored stone she was pointing at, held it up and studied it. "I'll be damned. Darned. I wonder."

"How can we tell?"

"I heard once the way to tell gold from the worthless stuff is to hit it with a hammer."

"You're joking."

"No, they say gold is a soft metal and it won't shatter." McCrea looked around. "Wish I had something to pound on it with."

"Would a rock do?"

"Maybe." He searched the creek bottom until he found a sandstone twice the size of his fist and rounded and smoothed by centuries of running water.

He carried it to a flat rock twenty feet from the stream. There, he placed his nugget on the flat rock and hit it sharply with the stone. "It shattered," he said, disappointed.

"No, not all of it." She was excited as she flicked away the shattered remnants of the nugget and picked up a tiny piece of gleaming metal. She turned it over, looked it over and handed it to him.

"Well, let's give it the old hammer test," he said, hopefully. Again the stone came down, this time hard enough to break the stone.

They both looked. The tiny piece of metal had flattened somewhat but had not broken. He picked it up. They stared at it and looked at each other.

Crystal Lee Brown whispered, "Gold."

"Lordy."

It was decision-making time again. They decided they could not stay there and hunt for more gold. "A man could get rich in a short time standing right here," McCrea said, "but if we stand here very long we might have to stay all winter."

Crystal Lee Brown shivered inside the ragged sheepskin coat. "It isn't worth our lives. Besides, spring will come again."

"Yeah. Let's saddle the horses and get on down the country while there's still some daylight."

They saddled up, with the remainder of their canned food rolled up in a blanket and tied on the packhorse. Just before they started to ride out they stopped and took a long look around.

"We have to pick out some landmarks so we can stake a claim," he said. "But that's easy."

"We can claim two sections, she said. "One for each of us. That will give us twice as much territory."

"We'll be sure to claim that place where the creek comes out of the hill and where it drops into the park. Back inside that hill is where the gold is, I'll bet." McCrea realized that he was talking like an excited kid. Grinning sheepishly, he took the packhorse's lead rope, wrapped it once around the saddle horn, passed the end under his right thigh to hold it, and led the way.

They rode past the cabin, and McCrea stopped, scanned the country and turned downhill. "If we're lucky, we'll find an easier way out of here than the way we came."

She scanned the terrain, too, trying to see over the next hill and over the trees. Suddenly, she inhaled sharply.

His head snapped around and he stared at her. "Huh?"

She pointed. "Over there. See? In the trees. A cave."

He looked. It was a cave in the side of a hill, a hill covered with a thousand pine trees and a million rocks. A mound of dirt and broken rocks stood just outside the mouth of the cave.

They rode over on a gallop and dismounted. McCrea peered inside.

"It doesn't go back very far, only about twenty feet." He fished a wooden match out of a shirt pocket and stepped inside. Striking the match, he held it out in front, then to one side.

"Crystal, come here."

She dismounted and hurried to him. He was staring down at another small stove, a few sticks of firewood, one can of beans, two dirty blankets, a few hand tools—and a wooden box.

The box had once been a tool box bound with thin strips of metal. It had no lid. Inside was a half-dozen canvas bags and they were full.

The match burned McCrea's fingers and he dropped it. He picked up one of the bags and carried it outside. The bag was tied with strong twine. He cut the twine with his pocketknife.

They both gasped.

"My God," she whispered.

"Lordy."

Four of the bags held nuggets, some as big as McCrea's thumb. The other two held gold dust which, they surmised, someone had taken from the bottom of the basin in the sluice box.

McCrea placed them carefully in the middle of a blanket, wrapped the blanket around them and tied the bundle on top of the packhorse's saddle.

They spoke little as they mounted up and rode away, now wanting to get as far from the mine as they could before dark.

The temperature had risen enough that much of the snow was gone from the ground by the time they got down to a lower valley. Only patches of it remained, but it made footing treacherous in places, and they rode knowing their horses could slip and fall at anytime.

Before dark, the sky to the north had cleared enough that they could see the top of Squaw Mountain, and they had hope that the sun would come out the next day.

It was not until they had hobbled the horses and opened two of the remaining six cans of beef and peaches that she mentioned what had been on her mind. But first she wanted to know whether he was thinking the same thoughts.

"How do you feel about it, Johnny? I mean, about finding Mr. Levi's mine.

McCrea chewed slowly, thoughtfully, before answering. "I feel good about it." He swallowed, put down the can he was holding and faced her. "I feel kind of unhappy, too. I keep thinking about Old Levi and his partner. How hard they worked. They dug some worthless holes before they struck a vein. They built that cabin with nothing but an ax and a hammer. They went through a lot to find gold. Now they're both dead and we've got the gold."

"It isn't fair, is it?" She was pensive, silent.

"Yeah," he said as he resumed eating, "but we had nothing to do with their deaths, and we can't bring them back." He forked another bite of canned beef into his mouth, chewed and then stopped chewing. "But I wonder if they've got any relatives."

"I've been thinking about that, too. What do you think we should do?"

"I don't know. That's something we'll have to give some more thought to."

"But, Johnny, what if we found out that one of them had a wife and family? What would you do?"

"Give it to them. Or maybe just half. What would you do?"

"I think we're entitled to half. But whatever you decide, Johnny, is fine with me."

The grass, the trees, everything was white next morning, but this time they were covered with frost instead of snow. The sky was clear, and Miss Brown allowed it was going to be a beautiful day when the sun came over the eastern hills. They ate sparingly, knowing they didn't have enough food to last until they got back to Bluebird.

"It's two more days to Old Shep's cabin and another day to town," McCrea surmised aloud. But he was feeling good. They were on their way back, the sky was clear, they had enough gold to buy just about anything they wanted, and it appeared that they had lost their pursuers.

"How much is gold worth?" he asked the young woman as they rode down a long ridge, looking for a way to get off it.

"I'm not sure, but I think I heard someone say it was worth about twenty dollars an ounce."

"Let's see now, we must have about twenty five pounds and there are sixteen ounces to the pound." He frowned as he tried to multiply the figures in his mind.

"About eight thousand dollars," Miss Brown said, "if it's pure gold."

"I'm betting it is. Old Levi wouldn't sack up anything else."

At one point, the ridge sloped down to a deep valley, and McCrea and Miss Brown turned their horses downhill. Again, they traversed the hill instead of sliding straight down. The horses were happy to be going down instead of climbing. At the bottom, they found themselves between two ridges where the traveling was easy, but they were going in the wrong direction. McCrea scanned the side of the hill to the west of them, trying to discover a way up. He lowered his gaze to the ground to rest his eyes and suddenly he reined up, studying the ground.

He looked behind them, turned his horse around and rode back a ways, then came forward again, eyes fixed on the ground. He rode on ahead, and finally turned back and looked up at Miss Brown. "I do believe we've found a trail."

"Really?" Her eyebrows arched and she looked down. "I don't see it. Oh yes, I think I do."

It was barely visible, but there were a few places where the tall, brown grass parted, and a close examination revealed packed dirt among the clumps of grass and rocks.

"It's an old trail," McCrea said. "Could be just a game trail, or it could be that old Ute trail I heard about."

"Will it lead us down?"

"I don't know yet. If it's the Indian trail, it'll take us all the way down to the foothills, but I don't know where it comes out of the mountains. It might come out a long way from nowhere."

"But wouldn't it at least follow an easier route?"

"Yeah. The Indians hunted in this country for many years. They would have found an easier route."

"Suppose it's not an Indian trail and is just a game trail?"

"Well, the deer and elk would probably have picked out the best way, but it would be the best way for them and not necessarily for men and horses."

"What do you think, Johnny?"

"We'll follow it if we can. That is, if it goes in the right direction. I hope it goes over that hill up there."

On they went, eyes to the ground. Twice, they had to stop and scan the ground carefully to keep on the path. When they came to where it widened as it crossed a creek, they knew they were on a trail that had been created by men and horses.

"Yep, it goes up that hill," McCrea said. "If we're lucky, it'll turn up there and go west down off the hill."

The trail went up along the side of the hill, above a rocky outcropping, into the timber, under a rock cliff and finally to the top. There, it turned back west, and McCrea was jubilant. "Yep. Whoever or whatever made this trail knew where they were going. They knew this country better than we do."

Miss Brown was jubilant, too. "We're safe now, aren't we, Johnny."

"Well," McCrea answered cautiously, "I can't say we're out of all danger. But I do believe we're better off now than we've been since this whole thing started."

"Know what I'm going to do when we get back

to civilization?"

He grinned at her, pleased to see her happy.

"I'm going to take a long bath in a large tub. A hot bath. And then I'm going to fix my hair. I must look a mess. What about you, Johnny?"

Grinning crookedly, McCrea ran a hand over his chin. "Reckon the first thing I'll do is shave. I must look like a porcupine."

She laughed for the first time since she had been taken kicking from her cabin in Bluebird, a long time ago. How long ago was it? Only a few days? It seemed like years. But it would soon be nothing more than a bad memory. They had found a trail that would lead them out of the mountains, perhaps down to the San Lomah Road, then to town. They would run out of food and they would be hungry, but they would get there. Yes, they were safe now. And they had gold.

For a moment, a sad thought crossed Miss Brown's mind again. They had found Mr. Levi's strike, and they had taken six bags of gold that he had accumulated, had worked for. Somehow, she felt that she and Mr. McCrea had no right to it. But if they didn't, who did? Relatives? Only if Mr. Levi or his partner left widows or orphaned children behind. If that was the case, she would give up at least half of her claim to it. Only half?

Well, she and Mr. McCrea, Johnny, had earned half. It was because of the lost mine that they had been put through a great deal of danger and suffering. He had been severely beaten, and she had been kidnapped and threatened with rape and torture. She was almost raped and would have been if he had not come along. Then they had been forced to flee to the higher mountains where they could have perished. All because of Mr. Levi's hidden mine. And now that they had accidentally found it; who was entitled to it?

Legally, she and Johnny McCrea were entitled to the gold. But Crystal Lee Brown knew that the law was not always just. And she knew that if there were widows and children she could not in good conscience keep all the rewards.

Best of all—and Miss Brown smiled to herself—Johnny apparently felt the same way. That was important, too. Very important.

Their stomachs were growling with hunger when they stopped for the night, and the handful of dried apricots and the tin of dried beef they shared failed to satisfy their appetites. But they were in good spirits. They felt safe enough to build a small fire and use the remainder of the coffee, and the chilly night made the fire feel cheery as well as warm.

They talked about numerous things, their voices low and intimate, and then came the question that McCrea knew would come sooner or later.

"I don't mean to pry, Johnny, and if you don't want to tell me about yourself you don't have to, but I'm bursting with curiosity."

When he didn't answer and only stared at the fire, she apologized. "I'm sorry."

Suddenly, he was talking. He was staring into the fire and he was talking as if he wanted her to know, as if he had to tell her. He told her about the ranch that started with his grandfather's homestead and then his father's, and grew as they were able to buy more land until they had twenty sections of good salt grass straddling the Pecos River in the Pecos Valley, New Mexico Territory.

He told her about growing up on the ranch, an only

child and a happy one, and—his voice slowed—about his mother's death of pneumonia right after his dad had built a two-story house for her.

Now his voice turned bitter as he told how cattle rustling got so bad some ranchers were being driven out of business, and how his dad's ranch was losing cattle rapidly. How it was common knowledge that three men were behind the rustling, but how the sheriff would do nothing, saying he had to have proof; how when rustlers were caught the so-called court of law set them free again when witnesses were scared off.

Still staring at the fire, McCrea's voice rose an octave, and he spoke faster as he told about the final blow. The ranch had lost so much stock to the thieves that they had nothing to ship that fall and were facing financial ruin. Then came the day that McCrea had spent riding the hills, searching the mesquites, hoping to find enough beeves to trade for winter supplies, coming home driving six head of steers and heifers ahead of him, stopping on a rise and seeing the smoke. He told of riding hard to the ranch, finding the house burned, finding his dad in the front yard shot through the lungs, unable to talk but able to scratch three names in the dirt. McCrea seemed to be talking to himself, reliving the experience, and his voice quickened as he told of burying his dad beside his mother and grandfather, riding to town, finding the three men in a saloon where he knew he would find them, and—

"Johnny. Johnny." She had to speak his name twice sharply before she was able to bring him out of his nightmare. "It's over, Johnny. It's in the past. I'm sorry I asked, Johnny. Please forgive me."

McCrea realized that he had talked more in the last ten minutes than he had in the previous year. But he had to tell her the rest. He had sold what stock he had left, all but two horses, and had put the land and buildings, what was left of them, up for sale. He had put his saddle on one horse and his bedroll on the other and had ridden north, trying to leave what had happened behind. His first stop was on a ranch near the Colorado border, and he was happy to be cowboying again, even though he was working for somebody else. But then he was recognized as "Johnny McCrea, The Fastest Gun in the West," and he had to move on. His next job was with the Diamond J, and he was planning to leave there soon and go back to Rosewell where he was ready to accept an offer from the Turkey Track outfit for his land.

His plans beyond that were vague, but he wanted to go far away.

Crystal Lee Brown moved closer and put a hand on his shoulder. "I understand. Believe me, I know what it is like to run."

Firelight flickered across her face as McCrea found himself looking into her brown eyes. He saw sympathy there and understanding. Had he talked too much? No, it was good to talk to somebody. Somehow he felt better. But there was trouble in her eyes, too. What was it? Sure, it was something in her past. It was obvious that she was hiding her past. Would she talk about it?

Crystal Lee Brown wanted to comfort the cowboy. She wanted to put her arms around him and hug him close, the way Aunt Agnes had hugged her when she was young.

"Johnny, I—" Should she tell him about herself? She wanted him to know. But perhaps this was not the right time. Perhaps there would be a better time. "Johnny, I'm glad you told me. It just makes me respect you even more. And I have a whole wide world full of respect for you, Johnny."

"Thanks for listening, Crystal." That was all he had left to say. He went to his blankets, pulled off his boots and turned in for the night.

It was noon the next day when McCrea again saw the short, lean man with the concha belt and the gimpy leg. The man had a rifle pointed right at him.

Chapter Nineteen

McCrea was angry with himself when it happened. He should have known or at least suspected it. How dumb can a man be? He and Miss Brown had eaten lightly, and he had smoked the last of his tobacco. They had resumed following the dim trail where it wound around hills, cliffs, and canyons. Their stomachs were growling with hunger, but they were in good spirits.

At noon they had stopped, loosened the cinches and allowed the horses to graze. "If they don't stay strong we'll never get back to town," McCrea had said.

They had stopped in a small grassy park near a narrow stream. On the other side of the stream huge boulders were piled as if the sky had dropped them there and let them stay where they fell. Miss Brown had excused herself and walked around the pile of boulders out of sight. While she was gone, McCrea had poked around and found a spot under an overhanging boulder where a few charred sticks and smoke-darkened rocks told him that someone had camped there many years earlier.

Squatting, McCrea had poked around in the dirt and

uncovered a broken arrowhead. Indians on a hunting trip had camped there, he mused, and one of them had had to replace the broken arrowhead. He had poked around in the dirt again, thinking he might find something else interesting, and heard her scream.

Afraid she had met a bear or cougar, McCrea splashed across the creek and ran around the boulders, looking for her. The only person he saw was the crippled man. He was grinning, and he had a rifle pointed right at McCrea's chest.

"One more step and you're dead, cowboy."

For a second, McCrea couldn't believe it. But when he thought about it he realized he had done something stupid. In fact, he had done several stupid things.

His eyes searched the terrain for Miss Brown, and the fear that was in his throat grew into a choking lump when he failed to see her.

Another man stepped around a boulder, carrying a pistol. It was the husky one who had accompanied the cripple back there near the town of Bluebird.

"Didn't think you'd ever see us again, did you?" The husky one was grinning, too.

"Where is she?"

"Oh, she ain't hurt," he said. "Not yet. But you're gonna be."

The crippled one was leaning, standing on his shortened right leg, and he chuckled. "We caught 'er with 'er bloomers down."

"Yeah." The husky was no longer grinning. His face was hard. "Just the way you left us. Now you're gonna pay for it." He raised the pistol and aimed it at McCrea's face. The hammer was back.

"Don't, you fool." The cripple had stopped smiling,

too, and was glaring at his partner.

"Why not? After what he done to us?"

"Huh." The cripple snorted. "You think I don't remember? I'm the one with two yards of tape around my chest. If we couldn't of made those miners think we was robbed, we'd of had a hell of a time. We'll have our fun, but not 'til he tells us about the gold."

The pistol did not waver. "Yeah. Go look at what's on that packhorse. I'll keep 'im covered."

The cripple glared at his partner a moment, then lowered the rifle and limped away toward the horses. The husky man grinned again. "Thought you done somethin' smart, didn't you?"

"No." Now that he was finally facing what he had been afraid of, McCrea felt no fear for himself, only for the young woman. "No, I didn't do anything smart. I'm so dumb I ought to be shot."

"Don't worry, you're gonna be."

"Miss Brown has done nothing to you. You've got no quarrel with her."

"She's seen us and she'll know us if she sees us again."

McCrea tried to think of a logical argument, but there was none. He and Miss Brown were as good as dead. The only question that remained was how much they would have to suffer before they died. She would suffer the most. Funny—McCrea grinned, rather he grimaced, when he thought of it—he was known as "Johnny McCrea, The Fastest Gun in the West," and here he stood with a six-gun on his hip, his hand only fifteen inches away from it, and he knew he could not draw and shoot fast enough. His antagonist would put a bullet into his brain if he made one move toward the gun.

As if he had read McCrea's mind, the husky man

ordered, "Turn around." McCrea did as ordered, and the man took his gun. The cripple limped back, excited.

"They've got gold. They found that mine."

McCrea turned, facing them again. "You'll never find it."

"Oh yes we will." The cripple unsheathed his bowie knife and limped over to McCrea. "You're gonna tell us all about it."

"Hell." McCrea snorted. "I could tell you nothing but lies, and you wouldn't know the difference."

It was true and the cripple knew it. He could force words out of anyone, but he would have no way of knowing whether the words were true.

"If you kill us," McCrea said, "you'll never find that mine. And if you torture us, we'll just make up a story."

The two hoodlums looked at each other, uncertain about what to do next. Finally, the husky one spoke. "How much gold they got on 'em?"

"A lot. I'll bet they've got twenty-five or thirty pounds."

The husky one whistled through his teeth. "That's a lot of gold. We could split that up and go a hell of a long ways."

"That's not what the boss wants. He wants that mine."

"Well, what the hell does he expect us to do? I ain't goin' back up there now."

"It ain't snowin' now, and whoever finds that mine is gonna get rich. Twenty-five or thirty pounds ain't nothin."

"The hell it ain't. We could split it three ways and be long gone before the boss knows what happened."

For the moment, McCrea was forgotten, and he weighed his chances of escape. He had no weapon, and he could not outrun bullets. The only way to escape was to overpower the two thugs. He had succeeded in doing that once with the help of a bronco horse, but now he had no help, and they would watch him more closely. Yes, they were watching him—arguing, but keeping a wary eye on him, too. Where was Crystal? One of them had mentioned splitting the gold three ways, and that meant there was a third man around somewhere, no doubt guarding her. And who was the boss?

"Well, I sure as hell ain't goin' back up there now," the husky one was saying. "It'd take two, three days to go back to where they came from, and another two, three days just to get down here again. And it's another two, three days to town. Hell, it could snow ten feet before then. Hell no, I ain't goin' back."

The cripple was suddenly pensive. Leaning to the right, he glanced at McCrea, then studied his boots. "Maybe we won't have to go back this year. Listen, we lost their sign way up there at the foot of that mountain, and they were headed north. All we have to do is go back up there next spring and go north from there, and I'll bet we'll find it."

Now the husky one was pensive. "Mebbe you're right. Hell, if we know about where that mine is, the boss'll have to keep us happy all winter so we can find it for 'im next spring."

The cripple chuckled. "With his money, he can make life mighty pleasant this winter."

"Yeah, he'll have to keep us happy."

They both chuckled, and they turned to McCrea. "That means we don't need you, cowboy." The husky one raised his pistol.

McCrea's lips turned up into a sneer. "I thought I was

dumb. Whoever your boss is he won't need all of you. Do you think he's going to pay to keep three of you all winter just so one of you can show him where you lost our trail?"

Before they could answer to that, the other man appeared out of a nearby gulch. It was the broad-shouldered Texan McCrea had let go back near Shep's cabin. "Ah got 'er tied up. She ain't goin' nowheres. What the hay-all're you two talkin' so much about anyways?"

McCrea answered. "They're trying to decide which of you will live long enough to get back to Bluebird and report to your boss."

"What the hay-all d'ya mean by tha-yet?"

"You tell him," McCrea said to the others.

The cripple was leaning on the rifle, his right hand over the bore. "Listen, Bert, we'd be fools to try to find that mine now, what with the snow and all, but we think we follered these two far enough that we can find it right after the spring thaw."

"Yeah, so wha-ut?"

"So we think maybe the boss'll want to keep us fat and happy this winter."

"Humph." McCrea snorted. "He only needs one of you. Which one will he pick?"

"Shut up." The husky one raised his six-gun again. "One thing is for shore, we don't need you."

McCrea tried to swallow back the fear. "There's something they didn't tell you, Bert. We've got about twenty-five pounds of pure gold over there. That's about eight thousand dollars' worth. They'd like nothing better than to split that money two ways and leave you out of it."

196

The cripple yelped, "That's a goddamn lie." He picked up the rifle and aimed it at McCrea's chest. "You spoke your last verse, cowboy."

The broad-shouldered Bert pushed the rifle aside. "Now just a gaw-ud damn minute."

Things happened swiftly then.

The husky one, feeling threatened, brought his gun barrel around in a wild roundhouse swing and knocked Bert to the ground. The cripple, muttering "No goddamn body pushes me, by God," swung his rifle barrel down and fired point-blank into Bert's chest.

McCrea charged. It was a desperation move, but it occurred to him in a flash that the two men had killed a partner, and they would not stop killing now.

He rammed his head into the husky man's face just as the hoodlum started to turn back. The blow would have knocked the husky one down had not McCrea grabbed him around the waist and swung him around facing his partner. The hoodlum was now between McCrea and the rifleman, and he was too groggy from the blow in the face to offer much resistance.

But the short, lean cripple was levering another shell into the firing chamber. He was about to shoot.

With strength born of desperation, McCrea threw the husky man at the crippled one. The cripple, already tilted to the right, was not able to stand up under the collision, and he hit the ground on his back with his partner on top of him. By the time he was able to struggle out from under him, he was looking up into the bore of a six-gun in John McCrea's hand.

The crippled hoodlum, now on his knees, let loose a string of obscenities. But his mouth was all that moved. If he had as much as moved one finger on the rifle, it would have been the last thing he ever did. The hammer was back on the six-gun McCrea held, and his finger was tightening on the trigger. Another ounce of pressure and the gun would fire, and the crippled man's life would end.

He ought to do it, McCrea told himself. This was the second time he had miraculously escaped death at the hands of these two, and he ought to kill them right now.

The thickset man started to pick himself up, and McCrea hissed through clinched teeth, "Stay down. Stay right there, you sonofabitch." The husky one immediately stopped moving.

But the short lean cripple was so frustrated and angry he didn't seem to care what happened. "Shoot," he dared McCrea. "Goddamn you, shoot."

McCrea looked down the short barrel of the six-gun that he had jerked out of the other man's hand and fixed the front sight right in the middle of the cripple's face, a face twisted and ugly with hatred. "Let go of that rifle."

For a long moment, the crippled man seemed undecided as to whether he wanted to obey or commit suicide by trying to bring the rifle up and shooting. It would be certain suicide, but for a long moment he seemed to be on the verge of trying it.

"Drop it." McCrea was also on the verge of doing something drastic. He was on the verge of firing a .45 slug into the face of a man who had twice intended to kill him, who had dragged him and cut him with a knife, who had forced him and Miss Brown to risk their lives trying to escape.

They glared at each other. Finally, the crippled man's fingers slowly released their hold on the rifle, and finally, the rifle was lying harmless on the ground.

"Now stand up. Both of you."

They stood up slowly, carefully, the cripple leaning to the right.

And now McCrea had another problem. He wanted to see to Miss Brown, and he didn't dare take his eyes off the two hoodlums. Without moving his eyes, he called to her.

"Miss Brown. Crystal."

Her answer came from somewhere a hundred feet or so behind him. "Johnny, are you all right?"

"I'm all right. Where are you?"

"I'm over here in a gully. I'm—I'm tied up."

"I'll be over there in a minute." To the two men, he said sharply, "Walk. In that direction. Wait. You, take off that gunbelt." The cripple unbuckled his gunbelt and let it fall from his hips to the ground. Now both men were unarmed. "Walk."

With the two men leading the way, McCrea went around back of the pile of boulders and found Miss Brown bound hand and foot in the sandy bottom of a shallow dry wash. Relief flooded her eyes when she saw McCrea behind the two men.

"Johnny. I heard a shot and I thought that you—I thought they had killed you."

She was sitting up with her ankles bound and her hands tied behind her. The baggy, ragged overalls she wore were twisted around her waist and knees, and the cutoff tail of her night dress and gown was outside the overalls.

"It's all right now, Crystal. They shot their partner, but now they're unarmed and harmless."

The sudden release from tension and worry brought a tear to her eye. "Thank God. I thought it was over for us."

Ordering the two men to lie facedown, McCrea lifted the bowie knife from the sheath on the cripple's left side and used it to cut the young woman's bonds. She stood up, rubbing her wrists.

"Did they hurt you?" he asked.

"No. They caught me completely unawares. Where did they come from?"

"Up ahead of us."

"But how—how did they get there?"

"It was my fault, Crystal. I just wasn't using my head."

"But how—"

"I can guess. The snow turned them around, the way I thought it might. When they found they couldn't follow our tracks they decided to go back. And like us, they tried to find an easier way back. Somehow they came out on the Ute trail, too, but up there somewhere." McCrea nodded in the direction they had been traveling. "If they had come out back there, we would have seen their sign. They had to have come out up ahead."

McCrea was watching the two prone men, and he shot a quick glance at Miss Brown. "I should have been more careful. They looked back and saw us. I was so busy trying to keep that trail in sight that I didn't see them. They backtracked to this pile of rocks and waited for us to come along."

Miss Brown straightened her clothes and pushed the cutoff tails of her nightdress and gown inside the waist of the baggy overalls. "And we played right into their hands by stopping here."

"I was dumb." McCrea shook his head sadly. "I almost cost us our lives."

She stood beside him and touched his left arm. "You're not dumb, Johnny. It was your outdoorsman-

200

ship and intelligence that have kept us alive this long, and we're still alive."

"We're lucky."

"But how—" She looked up at him. "How did you, uh—"

"They didn't trust each other. That gave me a chance."

"That shot I heard, they killed that other man?"

"Yeah."

She shuddered. "What are you going to do with them?"

"That ought to be easy. I ought to just shoot them and leave them here for the coyotes to clean up."

"Can you do that, Johnny?"

He wanted to assure her that he could not just shoot two unarmed men, but he didn't want them to know that. "One wrong move out of them and I'll kill them the way I would a rattlesnake."

Chapter Twenty

It was mid-afternoon before McCrea and Miss Brown resumed their journey. He had ordered the two hoodlums to bury their dead partner under rocks and had left them afoot, with no guns, but with the promise that he would leave their horses somewhere farther along.

"That could be the third mistake I made," he said to Miss Brown.

"What do you mean, Johnny?" She was riding easily, counting her lucky stars that she was still alive.

"The first was when I left them alive and free, though barefooted, back at Bluebird. The second was when I failed to watch for them on the trail ahead of us, and the third could turn out to be leaving them alive now."

The last handful of dried fruit and the last tin of dried meat was consumed that night. The night was clear and cold and the fire felt good as Crystal Lee Brown sat before it in her sheepskin coat with a blanket wrapped around her shoulders. It will soon be over, she thought. If they get going early next morning they should be back at Shep's cabin by early afternoon, and they should get back to Bluebird the next day. What would she do then?

Leave? She had plenty of money now. With the two thousand she got for her cafe and her share of the gold, and added to that her share of a valuable gold mine, she had more than enough money to go anywhere she wanted to go. Alone?

She glanced at John McCrea. He was staring into the fire and he, too, seemed to be lost in thought. What was he thinking about? Was it possible his thoughts included her?

"Johnny?"

He looked up, a question in his eyes.

"I'd like you to know about me. You have no doubt heard the rumors. I'd like you to know."

"I don't listen to rumors, Crystal, but I know you're worried about something."

How should she tell him? Where should she start? Would it make any difference? She had to know.

"Johnny, I—I've lived in a house—of prostitution."

"Huh?" He seemed surprised, even startled. His mouth opened as if he wanted to say something, but didn't know what to say.

"Yes. In Dallas, Texas. I was practically brought up in a house."

He stood up suddenly and stepped over to a large rock where he had left several dead tree limbs. He stomped on a piece of wood, breaking it into the right lengths, carried them to the fire and fed them to the flames.

"Let me start at the beginning, Johnny. You see my sister and I were raised by our father after my mother died giving birth to another child. Both my mother and the baby died. My, our father was an alcoholic. He was a good and religious man when he was sober, but he was mean when he drank."

"Crystal, you, I, uh—" McCrea shrugged.

"Hear me, will you, Johnny? You have to know. One night he came home drunk and beat me. My older sister and I waited until he fell asleep and we left. We walked all night, carrying two carpetbags with our belongings, and finally at daylight we got a ride in a wagon. We went to Dallas. We were so hungry that we stole food. My sister was caught and sent to reform school. I ran."

"I walked the streets two days without eating. And," Crystal Lee paused and said, "I saw a lady in a carriage, a beautiful lady wearing beautiful clothes. She saw me staring at her and called me to her. She asked if I was hungry and I told her I was. She took me home with her."

"Listen, Crystal, you don't have to talk about it."

"I do have to. She took me home with her. It was a large, beautiful house, and it wasn't until after we got there that I realized it was a, uh, you know. I was only fourteen. She took me in and treated me like a daughter. She bought me clothes and had a tutor come in to teach me reading and writing. She herself taught me how to run a kitchen and keep books. I called her Aunt Agnes. She was gentle and kind and never raised her voice to anyone. When a girl displeased her, she just sent the girl packing without any discussion."

McCrea cleared his throat. "She must be quite a woman."

"She was, Johnny. She ran the best house in Texas, and the men who came there were gentlemen of quality. Aunt Agnes kept me in my room studying most of the time, but I had to sneak a look now and then, and I knew what was going on."

"One evening when I was eighteen, Aunt Agnes

brought a young man to my room, a well-dressed and well-groomed young man from a very wealthy family."

Crystal Lee paused again and looked over at McCrea. He was listening, but his mouth was clamped shut.

"Aunt Agnes left us alone, and before she left she whispered that the young man was paying triple the usual fee. I knew what she expected of me, and I felt that I owed it to her. I—"

"That's enough." McCrea was looking hard at her. She forced herself to meet his gaze, her eyes pleading for understanding.

"Please, Johnny. I want you to hear it from me." When he said nothing more, she continued, "After all, I had lived with it so long that I thought it was the thing to do, I—" Her voice trailed off into silence. McCrea was staring at the fire again. After a long moment, she went on, speaking in a rapid monotone:

"One day Aunt Agnes went shopping and was killed by a runaway team. The horses and wagon all ran over her. I didn't know she was dead until the police came. Then her lawyer came and told me I was her only heir, that I had inherited the house. Next the police came again. Two of them. They made me understand that the house was illegal and if I was going to run it, I had to give them some money every Monday morning. I paid them. Then I decided to try to find my sister so I put ads in the newspapers until she finally called on me. She had married a Baptist preacher. When she saw what I was doing she prayed for my salvation, and she and her husband borrowed some money from me to build a new church. But pretty soon I realized I wasn't cut out for that kind of life. Besides I couldn't control the girls the way Aunt Agnes did. So I closed the house and sold it."

"I got a job in a bank and got along very well until I was recognized. Men began to whisper and smile at each other behind my back. I was fired. I was told that the bank didn't want anyone with my reputation in its employ. I didn't blame them, and I knew I had to go far away. I went all the way to Denver and got a job in another bank. For two years everything went well. But it happened again. I was recognized and had to leave again."

"I heard about the cafe for sale in Bluebird, and I thought I would be safe in a small ranch community like that. And I was for a year. Then gold was discovered, and men poured into town from everywhere and I was recognized. Now I have to move again."

She stopped talking suddenly and sat hugging her knees. McCrea stood up, broke another piece of deadwood and dropped it into the fire. His movements were quick, jerky, as if he was irritated at something.

Her heart sank. He was angry. She would rather die than have him disgusted with her, and she felt like crying. She put her face in her hands to hide the tears.

He paced back and forth behind her and finally began talking, as if to himself as much as to her. "I don't know what I'd have done. I never knew what it was like to be a homeless child and half starved. I might have done the same thing. I can see—anybody can see—you're trying to live it down. I never saw anybody work harder than you did at that cafe."

Squatting beside her, he put a hand on her shoulder. "Listen, I've admired you ever since the first time I saw you. The past is past." Gently, he took her hands in his and pulled them away from her face. "We've both been running from the past. It's time we quit running. We've got some thinking to do."

Crystal Lee wiped her eyes with the palms of her hands, and her voice was weak as she asked, "About what, Johnny?"

"About us."

This time they did their thinking out loud and together. When the fire died, they rolled up in their blankets. Only this time they slept in each other's arms.

About midnight, John McCrea awoke with a start and listened carefully. That footstep he heard, was it horses or human? He strained his ears while his mind raced. Did he do something dumb again? He had left two very dangerous men behind them. They were afoot and unarmed, but they could, by walking all night, have caught up with him and Miss Brown.

Slowly, carefully, McCrea slipped out of the blankets and pulled on his boots. The half-moon was high now, and it shed enough light that he could see the horses grazing, hobbled, nearby. He checked the guns. Three pistols and a rifle. They were all there. If the two hoodlums were nearby, they were still unarmed.

McCrea picked up the guns and carried them to a nearby boulder. He hid them under the boulder and took up a vigil on top of it. At daylight he was still there.

Food and coffee gone, there was no need to build a fire. McCrea hobbled two horses and left them where they would be found by the two men on foot. Then he and Miss Brown continued their journey.

"That might be dumb trick number four," McCrea said. "But I don't think that mean little jasper with the short leg would live long on one foot."

"At least they'll be a good long distance behind us,"

Miss Brown said.

"Yeah, that's what I'm planning on."

They rode out of the timber and into the valley shortly after noon but discovered they were far north of Shep's cabin. They switched directions and headed in the direction they knew the cabin to be. At mid-afternoon they saw it. There were horses in the sheep pen and smoke coming from the chimney.

McCrea reined up sharply. Miss Brown reined up beside him. "Who do you suppose is there?" she asked.

"I don't know. I see five horses in the pen."

"Could they be friendly?"

"Probably, but we can't be sure. I can't believe the gang of hoodlums is that big. We left one dead and two alive behind us. Five more would make it a small army."

"The sheriff, perhaps?"

McCrea sat his horse, eyes fixed on the cabin in the distance. "I wish I knew." Then suddenly, McCrea smiled as he saw a man come out of the cabin and bowleg his way to the pen. The man was thin, and twice on his walk to the pen he had to hitch up his pants.

Standing in his stirrups, McCrea took off his hat, waved it and let out a long southern yell. "Hoooeee. He-e-ey Jud. Hoooeee."

Judson Olesky's mouth dropped open beneath his handlebar moustache as he watched the two riders coming toward him on a gallop, leading two other horses. He turned back to the cabin and yelled, "Hyo-o-o in there. They're comin'. They're back."

Four men hurried out of the cabin, looked in the direction Judson Olesky was looking and watched the two riders come. McCrea and the girl rode up at a gallop, brought their horses to a stop and sat their saddles, smiling from ear to ear.

Olesky hitched up his pants and grinned back at them. "Danged if you ain't the sorriest-lookin' couple of culls I ever seen. Bail off them hosses and come in. Coffee's on."

Among the five men were two Diamond J cowboys, including Olesky, two townsmen, and Sheriff G.B. Harvey. The sheriff stepped up and shook hands with McCrea, politician style. "We were worried about you. We've been looking for you."

"We thought you two was feedin' the magpies by now," Olesky said grinning. "Where in the humped up— excuse me, ma'am—where in the world you been?"

The men had to be assured that Miss Brown was not hurt before they went into the cabin. A fire was burning in the stove, and a pot of coffee was boiling. "We was just fixin' to take on the last of the java," Olesky said. "Pull up a chair. Throw some of this down and then talk."

They drank black coffee and told all. They told about the cabin and the grave, the three gunmen, the death of one of them, and their escape. They talked excitedly about Old Levi's mine. McCrea went out and turned his horses into the pen, noticed that the grass was almost all cropped off, went back to the cabin and confronted the sheriff.

"What I don't understand, Mr. Harvey, is what took you so long to get here. Seems everybody in the county knew what was going on but you."

Sheriff G.B. Harvey pushed his white hat back on his head. "Now don't go blaming me, young fella. I didn't get back to Bluebird 'til yesterday and we don't have a telegraph yet. I couldn't go trailing off after you in the dark."

"Ever'body expected him back the day after I seen you," Olesky put in, "and I waited like a damn—excuse me, Miss Brown—like a fool for 'im. I finally got one of my men to come with me, and we been prowlin' all over up there lookin' for you. We was trackin' you right along 'til the snow hit. We seen where three others was trackin' you, too, and about all we could hope to do was catch up in time to pick up the pieces. And when the snowballs flew, all we could do was just hope you found that old Ute trail and got on over the divide."

G.B. Harvey spoke from the doorway where he was keeping a watchful eye to the north. "I got back from San Lomah after dark last night. When I heard what was going on, I deputized two men and got up here as fast as I could."

McCrea sat at the wooden table and rolled a cigarette with borrowed tobacco. He smoked quietly, then said, "It seems to me you should have come running when a woman was kidnapped. But—" McCrea took another drag on the cigarette, glanced at the grim-faced sheriff and back at his former boss. "Maybe you did the best you could. I don't know."

"Now don't you go blaming me, young fella. You aren't lilly white, you know. I suspected you right from the beginning, and you don't look any more innocent now."

Olesky stared hard at the sheriff. "How'd you figger that, Harv?"

"Mr. Harvey," Crystal said, anger causing her voice to rise, "how can you say a thing like that?"

McCrea took another drag on his cigarette but said nothing, waiting for the sheriff's explanation.

"His story is just too easy to make up," Harvey said.

210

"Everybody thinks Old Levi told him something about the location of his mine, and I think so, too. He found it, didn't he? He had to have some help from Miss Brown, but he went right to it, didn't he?"

No one answered, but two of the men shot curious glances at McCrea.

Harvey talked on. "He made sure everybody saw him in town when Miss Brown was kidnapped so he'd have an alibi, and he didn't wait for help but just went galloping off after her. He knew where to find her."

More curious glances were aimed at McCrea, but no one spoke for a long moment. The sheriff added, "He's a good actor but I've met good actors before."

"But," Crystal said, angrily, "what about those hoodlums we met up there? They intended to kill us both."

Shaking his head negatively, Harvey answered, "Did you hear any of their conversation? How do you know they weren't all thick as thieves, and he double-crossed them? Sure, that's what he intended to do, just grab all the gold he could carry and go on over the divide. If it hadn't been for a snowstorm, that's what he'd have done."

"It's not true." Crystal's voice was shaky with anger. "He risked his life for me."

"Oh, did he?" Harvey said. "He had two chances to shoot the men who kidnapped you and he let them go. He had a deal with them. And instead of coming back to town after he pretended to rescue you, he went straight to Old Levi's mine."

Tears of frustration came to Crystal's eyes as she yelled, "It's not true. It's a lie. We couldn't have gone back to town. We had to go the other way."

The sheriff shook his head negatively. All eyes were on McCrea. McCrea shook his head negatively, too, and spoke quietly. "We weren't looking for gold. All we wanted to do was save our hides."

Olesky hitched up his pants. "It could've been the way he said, Harv."

"Yeah, and it could have been the way I just said. We all know that Old Levi was tortured by somebody that wanted to find out where his mine is. This young fella is the last one to see him alive, and this young fella found the mine. Now doesn't that make you all suspicious?"

No one spoke for a long moment, then one of the townsmen deputies looked down at his boots and said, "Aw, I don't know what to believe. This is the damnedest—excuse me, Miss Brown—dangedest puzzle I ever heard of."

Olesky put a callused hand on McCrea's shoulder. "The law says a man is innocent until proved guilty. If I was on the jury I'd find him innocent."

"Yeah," said the Diamond J cowboy, "you've got a lot of suspicions but no proof, shurff. Johnny's a good hand and a good man."

Crystal wiped her eyes with the palm of her left hand and forced calmness into her voice. "All you've done since Johnny found Mr. Levi is try to blame him for everything that happened. You haven't even tried to identify the real killers." She was staring straight into Harvey's eyes. "What we ought to do is go back to town and put our heads together and see if we can figure all this out, instead of—" Her voice hardened a shade. "Just talking nonsense."

"I agree with Miss Brown, Harv," Olesky said. "Let's think this over and ask a lot of questions of a lot of people, and then if Johnny did it, I'll be as quick to string 'im up as anybody."

Harvey shrugged finally and let out a long sigh. "All right. But I'm offering him the same deal as before. I won't lock him up if he stays in town, but if he turns up missing, I'll have every lawman in the west looking for him.

"And I'll tell you all something else," the sheriff added. "When elections are held in this county I won't be a candidate. You can get somebody else to do your sheriffing."

"That's too bad, Harv," the Diamond J cow boss said. "I can't say I blame you. Now then," he said to McCrea, "do you think your hosses can make it on down to town tonight? There'll be a three-quarter moon, and it won't be so dark. And come to think of it, you didn't ride up here in the dark, did you?"

McCrea shook his head. "I just pointed that bay horse of mine in the right direction and let him find the way. Good thing he's never had a home in this part of the country or he'd have taken me there."

Olesky chuckled. "I always did say a horse has got more sense than a man." He hitched up his pants. "How do you feel, Miss Brown? Would you rather wait 'til mornin'?"

"I can stand it if the horses can."

"Wa-al," Olesky drawled, "they'll be mighty leg weary, but they'll live over it, and they can rest for a long time after tonight."

Sheriff G.B. Harvey was standing in the open door again, looking up at the higher country. He shot a scowl at McCrea. "How far behind do you think those two fellas are?"

"Anywhere from five to ten hours. That man with a short leg can't walk too fast."

"Well, I'll have to stay here and wait for them. Right here is the best place to arrest them. You say they aren't armed?"

"No. Their guns are out there with our saddles."

G.B. Harvey lifted his pearl-handled, silver-plated gun from its holster, checked the cylinder and replaced it. "Well, I'll wait for them. The rest of you can go on back to town."

The two townsmen deputies volunteered to wait with him. "No," the sheriff said, "if they aren't armed I can handle it by myself."

One of the deputies, a lanky man with a long sad face, insisted on staying. "I vowed, when you deputized me, to see this through."

"All right, Bud, stay if you want. How about you, Samuel?"

"I'll stay, too," said the other townsman deputy.

"Let's go out and bring all those guns in here," Harvey ordered. "And," he said, scowling at McCrea, "you'd better be in town where I can find you when I get there."

Chapter Twenty-One

It was a bone-weary Crystal Lee Brown who rode with three men into the town of Bluebird that moonlit night. The town was dark and the streets were deserted. A dim light came from The Palace, however, and a man who could be seen only by the glowing end of his cigarette saw them coming. He went into the saloon and spread the word.

A small crowd of drinkers and gamblers gathered in the moonlight to watch them come. Among them was the six-foot-six Amos Tarr. He smiled broadly, tipped his hat at Miss Brown and gallantly held her horse by the bridle while she dismounted.

"I know you need rest, Miss Brown, and I know your cabin is no longer fit for habitation. May I offer you my room for the night?" Before anyone could answer, he added hastily, "Alone, of course. I'll spend the night elsewhere. You can lock the door."

Crystal Lee looked at John McCrea for approval or disapproval. He nodded affirmatively. She asked, "Where will you sleep, Johnny?"

"Don't worry about me. I've got a bedroll somewhere."

"There's plenty of hot water at the hotel, and you can use the bathing facilities if you care to, Miss Brown." Amos Tarr was smiling pleasantly, towering over everyone else.

Crystal Lee sighed. "Oh, I'd certainly like a bath. And some clean clothes."

Several of the men were eying the packhorse, and two men stepped up and ran their hands over the lumpy load. "You wouldn't have gold under that blanket, would you?" asked a short plump man in a wrinkled business suit.

For a moment, McCrea did not know what to say. An honest answer would start a new wave of excitement in the town, and men would be risking their lives to find the place the gold came from. But that could not be prevented. The land recorder's office would be open in the morning, and he and Miss Brown could file a claim. The lost—and found again—mine would be safe. "Yeah, that's what it is."

"The hell you beller." A whiskered gent stepped up. "You found Ol' Levi's mine, didn't you?" His voice was accusing. "You knew all along, didn't you? 'Twixt you and her you knew where to look."

"No." McCrea sighed wearily. "We didn't know. We found it by accident."

"The hell you beller, you—" The whiskered gent did not get to finish his sentence. Amos Tarr stepped up next to him.

"Don't you dare make any accusations, mister. These people are very tired. They need rest. I'm sure they came by that gold honestly."

The whiskered gent gulped and kept quiet.

McCrea accompanied Miss Brown to her cabin, lit a lamp for her and stood by while she gathered a complete change of clothing. He walked back to the hotel with her where Amos Tarr was waiting. The tall man handed her a key. "Lock the door behind you, Miss Brown, and make yourself at home. Stay as long as you like. I'll sleep elsewhere."

"Thank you, Mr. Tarr. I certainly appreciate this."

Tarr supervised while the gold was placed in the hotel safe, and a receipt was made out to John McCrea. Then the riders led their horses to Johnson's Corrals. They had to yell and pound on the door to get Johnson out of bed. He opened the door to his two-room cabin near his corrals and barn, grumbling and fastening the suspenders of his overalls. When he saw who was there, he grumbled again, but told the men where they could corral their horses and where they could find feed for them.

"We ought to get on back to the wagons," Olesky said, "but I don't think that old pony of mine can make it tonight."

"Mine has gone about as far as he can go for awhile," McCrea said. "I sure owe him a long rest."

Olesky pulled a worn cowhide wallet out of his pants' pocket, fingered the bills in it, and decided he'd go back to The Palace and get into that poker game. The cowboy went with him. McCrea went looking for the bed he had been forced out of at gunpoint long ago. He found it where he had left it on the side of the grassy hill. He shook out the blankets to rid them of any small creatures that might have set up housekeeping in them, then pulled off his boots and crawled between them. Within ten minutes, he was sound asleep.

The warm water felt wonderful, and Crystal Lee Brown soaked in the long tin tub in the bathroom down the hall from Amos Tarr's room. She almost choked when she started to doze off in the water. With her reddish brown hair piled on top of her head, she stepped out of the tub, toweled herself dry, and put on the clean nightgown she had brought to the hotel with her.

The room Amos Tarr had loaned her was clean and airy and neat. His clothes hung neatly on a rack in the corner, and his shaving equipment, a straight razor and lather mug, had been placed on a small table beside a large china washbasin. A long rifle with fancy engravings on the stock and plate hung on a wall. Sighing pleasantly, she allowed herself to sink into the soft bed. Her stomach reminded her that she needed food, but she was too tired to worry about that.

Hours later a soft knocking on the door awakened her. She opened her eyes and was surprised to find herself surrounded by four walls. Sunlight was pouring into the room through the curtained window. It took a moment, but she finally realized where she was, and she smiled to herself. What an adventure. But it was over and she was safe. Not only was she safe, she owned a half-interest in a valuable gold mine, and—was it really true?—she had found her man.

The knocking persisted, and a soft voice came through the door. "Miss Brown. Miss Brown."

Crystal Lee recognized the voice of Maudie, and she got out of bed, slipped on a robe and went to the door. The two women fell into each other's arms, too emotional to speak. Finally, Maudie held Crystal at arm's length, her brown eyes shining, her black face smiling. "I heered you was back and safe, Miss Brown. It's a miracle. I just knowed they carried you off and killed you and I'd never see you again."

"I'm safe, Maudie."

"Was it just turrible, Miss Brown?"

"It was at times." Crystal Lee's lips turned up into a small smile. "And it was kind of wonderful, too."

Maudie's face went blank for a moment, and Crystal guessed that she did not understand. Then a frown appeared on the strong black face. "You must be hongry as a pet bear. You come on over to the cafe with me, and I'll fix you a breakfast that won't quit."

"I am famished. Let me slip on some clothes and I'll be right there."

He had not shaved in—Lordy, how long?—and John McCrea wanted to get cleaned up a little before he faced Crystal Lee Brown again. Though his stomach was constantly reminding him he needed food, he went to the cot house and shaved and washed out of a tin pan the best he could. He put on the cleanest clothes he had in his warbag before he went to breakfast. What he needed first was food and a lot of it, and then a hot bath and some clean clothes.

McCrea looked after his horses, pitched some hay to them, and went to the Bluebird Cafe. As usual, the cafe was crowded with miners and prospectors. They were talking excitedly about the woman and the men who had ridden into town late the night before with a packhorse-load of gold. The most often spoken words were "Levi's mine." But when McCrea walked in conversation ceased, and everyone stared silently at him. Everyone but Amos Tarr.

The tall man was seated alone at a table for four even though other men were standing and waiting their turn to sit. When he saw McCrea, Amos Tarr beckoned him over and invited him to take a seat.

"As the new owner of this enterprise, I have reserved a table for myself and my friends," he explained. "I'm happy that you came along. I have a business proposition for you."

McCrea appreciated being invited to sit at the table, but he only half listened to what the tall man was saying. His eyes studied the handwritten menu on the wall. A waiter with a smudged white towel around his middle and slicked-back hair came up and glanced at Amos Tarr and then waited expectantly for McCrea's order.

"There'll be a little delay, gentlemen," the waiter said. "Our cook heard about the folks that came in last night, and she dropped everything and went to the hotel."

Amos Tarr smiled. "Well, we'll forgive Maudie this time, William. She has been worried sick about Miss Brown. The events of last evening are good news for everyone."

"I'll fix your order special, Mr. McCrea," the waiter said.

"How are you fixed for eggs?" McCrea asked.

Amos Tarr answered, "We've got a few reserved for special folks, and you're special."

"Well, give me a couple of fried eggs and some bacon, lots of bacon, and a few flapjacks. And coffee."

"Yes sir." The waiter left but returned almost

immediately with a mug of steaming coffee.

"Now," Amos Tarr said, clipping off the end of a black cigar with a small silver clipper, "let's talk business."

McCrea took a sip of the coffee. It was mighty good. He could guess what the tall man was about to say, and he was only mildly interested.

"You're no miner." Amos Tarr lit the cigar and blew smoke at the ceiling. "You're a cattleman, and you no doubt are willing to sell that mine and go back south. What are you asking?"

The coffee was strong and scalding hot. Nothing could have tasted better. "I haven't thought about it, Mr. Tarr. I don't know what it's worth."

"Make a guess. Name a figure."

"It isn't all mine, you know. Miss Brown is part owner."

"Sure, but I'm guessing that she will agree to any deal you want to make."

Another sip of the coffee. "And there's the possibility that Old Levi and his partner, whoever he was, had heirs."

"I'm no lawyer, Mr. McCrea, but I do know that no claim has ever been filed on that mine. Only you and Miss Brown know where it is. You file a proper claim and you two will be the legal owners, heirs or no heirs."

McCrea was hesitant. The tall man had guessed right about one thing: He was no miner and didn't want to be. And he did want to go back to the Pecos Valley. But a worrisome thought kept tugging at his mind. He was a murder suspect. He couldn't leave town.

"Ten thousand dollars," Amos Tarr said and leaned back and watched McCrea's face to see if the figure had an impact. "That will buy a lot of land and a lot of cattle,

221

Mr. McCrea."

McCrea sipped the coffee. He was feeling a little weak from the lack of food, and he wished the waiter would return.

"I'll give you my note for ten thousand dollars." Amos Tarr leaned forward and put his elbows on the table. "That will be the quickest and easiest money you will ever make."

"I don't know, Mr. Tarr. I don't know what a gold mine is worth. I'll have to think about it."

"It's a good offer, Mr. McCrea. That mine sounds like a very good one, but its remoteness makes it difficult to mine. It can be worked only during the summer—about three or four months out of the year—and the ore will have to be transported on pack animals."

A platter of eggs, bacon, and pancakes was set before McCrea, and he wasted no time in pouring syrup over the pancakes and digging in. He had to force himself to chew slowly and thoroughly and not to make a hog of himself. His stomach seemed to want food faster than he could chew and swallow. Amos Tarr waited patiently.

Finally, McCrea looked up. "Your note, you said?"

"Yes. But don't worry, it's good. The new bank will open here in a few days, and I will immediately open an account with a draft on my bank in St. Louis. My notes can be quickly converted to cash."

McCrea met his gaze for a moment, then looked down and concentrated on eating.

"Fifteen thousand. How's that. Within a few days you can have fifteen thousand dollars cash in your pockets. Think of that, will you?" The tall man blew smoke at the ceiling and seemed to be studying the ceiling when he added, "There is something else you might consider. You are going to sell the property to someone and—" He looked McCrea in the eye. "You owe me, remember?"

"Yeah, I remember very well, Mr. Tarr. I'd be rotten meat now if it wasn't for you. But—" Again that worry entered his mind. "I'll think about it."

"You think about it and talk it over with Miss Brown, but I would like to have an answer by this evening. You can be on the stage tomorrow, a wealthy man. What do you think of that?"

Before McCrea could reply, the door opened and again all conversation ceased as Crystal Lee Brown and Maudie came in. Maudie hurried to the kitchen, and Crystal smiled broadly when her eyes picked McCrea out of the crowded room. McCrea and Amos Tarr stood, and the tall man pulled a chair out away from the table for her.

She glanced at him and concentrated on McCrea. "My, you look fresh this morning, Johnny."

"You too, Miss Brown. Crystal. How do you feel?" All the attention coming their way was embarrassing to the cowboy.

"Famished, but otherwise very good. I had a good sleep, thanks to Mr. Tarr." She sat, and Amos Tarr pushed the chair in for her.

"I'm happy I could do something for you, Miss Brown. You keep the room for as long as you want. I'll find other quarters."

"That is very kind of you, but I don't want to put you out anymore. I think I can have my cabin fixed today."

"If that is what you wish, Miss Brown, I will see to it personally. Now, we have some eggs reserved for special guests such as you and Mr. McCrea."

Crystal looked around at the men staring at her and at the doorway to the kitchen. "It feels strange, sitting here in my own—what used to be my own—cafe, waiting for service. I have an urge to go to the kitchen and get to work."

Amos Tarr threw his head back and laughed loudly. "You just sit right there and let someone wait on you for a change, Miss Brown. With your resources, you should become accustomed to being waited on."

The waiter appeared, and Crystal Lee ordered the same things McCrea had on his plate. McCrea's stomach tried to persuade him to resume eating, but he would have felt awkward and guilty eating before her food arrived.

She guessed what he was thinking. "Please, Johnny, don't let your breakfast get cold. I won't mind."

He noticed it when she first came in, and he was even more aware of it now: She was lovely. Her reddish brown hair was combed down to her shoulders, and her freshly scrubbed face had a light tan from the mountain sun. Her brown eyes sparkled. When she smiled, her teeth were white and even.

And she could not take her eyes off him. She wanted to touch him, to show affection, but she knew it would embarrass him. All she could do was smile, happy to be alive and with the man she loved.

Amos Tarr looked from one to the other and cleared his throat. "I, uh, I would like to talk business, but I have a feeling—in fact I know that this is not the proper time. If you will excuse me, I have some other business to take care of." He stood, towering above the table. "Please stay as long as you like. Use this table and this place as though it were your own."

She glanced up quickly. "Thank you, Mr. Tarr." Amos Tarr put on his high beaver hat and left.

When her food came, Crystal Lee ate quietly and

daintily but wasted no time with conversation. McCrea finished his meal and watched her eat. His coffee cup was refilled by the waiter. He sipped quietly until she finished her meal, leaned back in her chair and let out a long sigh.

"Ohhh, that was wonderful. I can feel the strength coming back. How do you feel, Johnny?"

Grinning, he said, "Fine." He glanced around the room, saw that they were no longer the center of attention, and added in a low voice, "You look wonderful. You're the prettiest gal this old cowhand has ever seen."

For a moment they sat, smiling at each other, but then they were interrupted. A man and a woman approached their table. The man was short and husky in baggy bib overalls. The woman was plump and plain in a plain cotton dress. Her hair was combed straight back and tied in a bun.

Chapter Twenty-Two

"I heered ya was back ta town," the man said as he and the woman arrived at the table. "An' I heered ya come back rich."

"Howdy, Mr. Henessy," McCrea said, standing. "Yeah, we're back." The two men shook hands.

"Nice to see you, Mr. Henessy," said Crystal Lee, nodding.

"Like ya ta meet my woman, Marylou." Arkansas Henessy put his hand on the woman's shoulder. "Finally got 'er ta come out here an' hep me spend some money."

As plain as she was, the woman had a pleasant smile, and her eyes danced merrily. She and her husband were invited to occupy the other two chairs at the table, and more coffee was served. Mrs. Henessy looked around the cafe and said she would like to own it.

"Yeah, she's worked all 'er life, an' she jest cain't set still and do nothin'," her husband said. "But I heered ya already sold it to that eastern financyoor."

"Yes. I wish I had known you were coming, Mrs. Henessy."

"Not ta change the subject," Arkansas Henessy put in, "but I 'spect ya're itchin' ta git over to the land office an' file yer claim."

"No hurry," McCrea said. "That mine is safe for awhile."

"Well, if ya don't mind my askin', what're yer plans?"

Thinking of the future brought back that nagging worry, and McCrea's answer was slow in coming. "Well, we're hoping to go back to the Pecos valley. That sheriff did one good thing for me. He kept me from selling my land. That would've been the worst mistake of my life."

Arkansas Henessy tamped tobacco into his corncob pipe but did not light it. "Well, that brings up another question. What're ya agoin' ta do about yer mine?"

"It's for sale," McCrea answered. "I'm no miner."

"Figgered ya wasn't."

Crystal Lee could see that Arkansas Henessy wanted to light his pipe put was afraid of offending her. "Go right ahead and smoke, Mr. Henessy. I don't mind."

He struck a match on the button of his suspenders, held it over the pipe and drew heavily until he got it smoking. "Ya're mighty nice folks, both of ya, an' I'd like to work out a deal with ya." He saw interest in McCrea's face and went on. "I could buy the mine, but that'd be kinder foolish since I ain't seen 'er and ain't agoin' ta see er 'til next spring. But from what I heered, she's a good un, and I'd shore like ta see 'er." He smoked, and McCrea and Crystal Lee waited to hear what else he would say.

"Now I know gold an' I know minin'. Been adoin' 'er er many a long yar. What I'd like ta do is work that mine n shares. That way nobody gits stung if she peters out, n' nobody gits cheated if she's as rich as they say she is."

227

"Sounds interesting, Mr. Henessy," said McCrea.

"Call me Arkansas, or Arky. Ever' time somebody calls me mister, I cain't hep alookin' behind me ta see who they're atalkin' to."

McCrea had to chuckle. "Arkansas it is."

"How 'bout fifty-fifty? You come back up here next spring and show me where it is, an' I'll git some men and go ta work. If that vein is as good as they think she is, we'll all make money."

McCrea turned to Crystal Lee. "How does that sound to you? We've been offered fifteen thousand dollars for it already."

"By whom?"

"Amos Tarr. He's ready to sign over another of his notes."

"That gentleman's a wheeler-dealer," Henessy said. "I just agreed to buy his hotel before it's finished. At his profit. That gentleman knows how ta make a buck."

McCrea chuckled. "Nothing wrong with that if you can do it."

"I like Mr. and Mrs. Henessy," Crystal Lee said. "This way if any heirs turn up, we can share the profits with them."

"Heirs?" Arkansas Henessy asked. "Did Ol' Levi have some kin folk?"

"Not that we know of," Crystal Lee answered, "but that is a possibility. We have decided that if he or his partner left a widow or children, we would like to share the proceeds with them."

Henessy grinned. "Yep, you're my kind of folks. But," he said, his eyes narrowing, "if the word gits out, ever con man and woman'll be aheadin' fer Bluebird."

228

"That could be a problem," McCrea put in. "Best thing to do is keep it quiet, just between us. And if anybody does show up and looks honest, let us know."

Grinning again, Henessy drawled, "Yep, that's the best thing ta do. An' I'll tell ya, folks, I been aknockin' aroun' this old country fer a long time, an' I met all kinds of people. When it comes ta judgin' people I'm hard ta fool."

Crystal Lee laughed a quiet, happy laugh. "We're going to love having you and Mrs. Henessy for partners, aren't we Johnny?"

"Shall we have a paper drawn up?" McCrea asked.

"Like I just said, Johnny, I'm hard ta fool. There ain't no lawyer aroun' here nohow. I'm ready ta shake on it." He held out a callused hand. They shook.

With a borrowed saw and hammer, McCrea fixed the door to Crystal Lee's cabin, then they went to the land office and filed their claims. Their next stop was at the hotel where they sold their gold to a buyer from Denver.

McCrea then went to the dry goods store where he bought a new plaid shirt, a pair of the new Levi's, socks, and underclothes. Back at the hotel, he offered the desk clerk five dollars to allow him to use the bathing facilities. The clerk glanced around to see if the conversation had been overheard, then hastily stuck the money in his pocket. McCrea bathed and put on the new clothes. He hesitated before buckling on the gunbelt. He didn't need a gun anymore. Or did he? If he hadn't got his hands on a gun back there when he found the dying prospector, he'd be dead himself. Somebody had tried to kill him. And he was still a murder suspect.

It was late afternoon when Sheriff G.B. Harvey rode in.

The sheriff was accompanied by the two townsmen deputies and the two hoodlums. As they rode down Main Street, the short, lean cripple's eyes shot fire at all the onlookers while the husky, bull-necked man looked down and refused to meet anyone's gaze. The hands of both men were tied to their saddle horns.

While they dismounted near The Palace, the sheriff was complaining. "I don't know how I'm supposed to keep prisoners with no jail. I'm going to have to put them in one of these cabins and keep a guard on them all night. And I'll have to take them to San Lomah on the stage in the morning."

A small crowd had gathered and questions were being asked. "Is that the ones that killed Old Levi?" someone asked. "Yep," said the whiskered gent. "I seen 'em around town and I never seen 'em doin' any work."

"That crippled feller's a mean one," another put in. "I seen him in jail at San Lomah when I was arrested for fightin'. I'll bet they're the ones that kidnapped that purty woman, too."

The crowd parted to allow a tall man to step forward. Amos Tarr stopped in front of the sheriff. "Congratulations, Mr. Harvey. You and your deputies are to be commended. You rode a long way to capture these two. I'm sure someone will volunteer the use of his cabin for the night."

"You can have mine," said the townsman deputy named Bud. "Just for tonight. I can bunk somewhere else."

"I'll need some volunteers to stand guard."

"You won't need no guards," said the whiskered gent. "We know what they done. We can hang 'em right now." He got some murmurs of agreement, but the tall man quickly put a stop to that.

"Now, gentlemen, that is not the way to do it. I understand there is a very good court of law in San Lomah, and the judge is extremely harsh. Justice will be done."

"That's right," G.B. Harvey said, "and I can't allow anyone to mistreat my prisoners."

John McCrea, seeing the crowd, sauntered over. He was quickly recognized by the whiskered gent. "Are they the ones, McCrea? Are they the ones that killed Old Levi and kidnapped that woman?"

"Yes and no," answered McCrea. "They're the ones who gave me a hard time, but it was cohorts of theirs who kidnapped Miss Brown." McCrea studied the crowd. "There's another one somewhere. A man with a scar on his face. He was one of the two kidnappers. The other one is dead."

"I seen that scar-faced galoot," the whiskered gent said. "I seen 'im just yestiddy."

"Where?"

"I seen 'im in The Palace eatin' ham sandwiches."

"Have you seen him today?"

"No, not today. But he's around here somewhere."

McCrea turned to the sheriff. "Wherever he is, he's dangerous. I left him afoot near Shep's cabin, and I guess he managed to walk back to town."

"We'll find him," G.B. Harvey muttered. He scowled at McCrea. "In the meantime, you stick around."

231

"Why is that, shurff?" the whiskered one asked. "Was he in on it? Is that how he found the gold?"

"He went right to it, didn't he?" Harvey answered. "That's all I'm going to say now, but I just might take him to San Lomah, too."

An angry murmur went through the crowd, but then Amos Tarr spoke again. "That's hard to believe, Mr. Harvey. He's a cattleman, not a gold hunter."

"He'd just better not leave town," Harvey said.

The prisoners were led away, and the crowd went back inside The Palace. McCrea stayed on the boardwalk. Amos Tarr stayed with him.

"Have you reached a decision?" he asked.

"Yes, Mr. Tarr. Crystal, uh, Miss Brown and I have decided to deal fifty-fifty with Arkansas Henessy."

Amos Tarr's face was suddenly drawn, with a tightness around the mouth. "I'm disappointed."

"I owe you my life, Mr. Tarr, and I'd like to find a way to repay you. But I only own a half interest in that mine. Crystal and Mrs. Henessy got to be friends in a hurry."

"I thought we were friends, Mr. McCrea, but now—" Amos Tarr turned and walked into the saloon.

McCrea watched him go and couldn't help feeling a pang of guilt. Amos Tarr had saved his life and now he was refusing his business offer. He should have accepted. He should have taken Amos Tarr's note for fifteen thousand dollars. Friends were supposed to trust each other, and Amos Tarr was a gentleman.

Deep in thought, he walked down the boardwalk toward Crystal Lee's cabin.

Crystal Lee worried about him. He was strangely silent through the supper she had cooked in her cabin. She knew him well enough to know he had something on his mind. "Since we are soon to become lifetime partners, Johnny, shouldn't we confide in each other? What kind of wife will I be if my husband can't confide in me?"

He grinned weakly. "You're right. I didn't want to worry you. It's just that this thing isn't over. I'm suspected of torture and murder, and we can't leave town until the real killer is identified."

"But I know you're innocent and so does everyone else who knows you."

McCrea shook his head. "I'm a stranger in town. The sheriff made a little speech in front of The Palace awhile ago, and now he's got others suspicious."

Crystal Lee was pensive, a frown wrinkle between her eyes. "What do you think, Johnny?"

"I've been thinking and thinking, and I'm not sure about anything. Except that there are more of these hoodlums around than the sheriff has in custody."

Crystal Lee's eyes widened. "Oh yes, I had thought of that. The scar-faced man who assaulted me up there, he got away. But he surely wouldn't come back here. And what can he do?"

"There's still another. You said the men who kidnapped you mentioned their boss?"

"Yes."

"Well, the two who dragged me away mentioned a boss, too. In fact, everybody mentioned the boss."

"Who do you suppose he could be?"

"I don't know, but I have this feeling that he'll crop up."

"Why don't you report this to the sheriff? It's his responsibility to worry about things like this."

McCrea reached a decision. "You're right. I'll go hunt him up right now."

"While you're gone I think I'll go over to the hotel. I have seen how easy it is to break into this cabin, and I don't want to keep this money here. While you're gone I'll take it to the hotel and place it in the safe."

"Good idea."

It was after sundown when McCrea walked to the home of Sheriff G.B. Harvey, and a cold wind blew down from the high peaks to the north. A few snowflakes sailed almost horizontally. McCrea pulled his hat down tighter and turned up the collar of his duck jacket. It would be good to get back to Southern New Mexico Territory, back to where people weren't always looking at the sky and wondering if they were going to be snowed in.

He wondered how long he and Crystal would have to stay in town, and whether they would have to go to San Lomah to testify at the trial of the sheriff's prisoners. That is, if he could clear himself of the crime. He had heard of lawyers using legal maneuvers to keep a trial going for so long the jury became weary and was willing to accept almost anything.

But he was sure Crystal would agree that they had to do what they could to help bring justice to the West.

The same hard-faced, grey-haired woman answered his knock on the door. "Mr. Harvey is out taking his turn guarding his prisoners. He won't get much sleep until they are locked up at San Lomah."

"Thank you. I'll try to find him."

He was half a town block from The Palace when he saw one of the deputies walking toward him. Before the two men could meet, the deputy turned in through the saloon doors, and McCrea followed.

"Evening, Mr. McCrea." The deputy was the lanky, sad-faced one named Bud. He had a week's growth of whiskers and ragged holes in the elbows of his plaid mackinaw.

"Evening."

"Thought I'd have a little eye-opener before I took my turn at guard. Believe me, I haven't had much sleep lately."

"I know how it is," McCrea said. "Let me buy you one."

"Sure 'nuff."

The whiskey was delivered by the bartender with the rolled-up sleeves. McCrea and the deputy threw the whiskey down their throats in one gulp. The deputy blinked and said, "I see you're carryin' out the sheriff's orders by stayin' in town."

"Yeah. Listen, I'd like to ask you something. You were deputized, weren't you?"

"Yup."

"Then you have the power to make an arrest?"

"Yup, but if you want somebody arrested, I'd rather the sheriff done it. I ain't a regular deputy, and I ain't ever arrested nobody."

McCrea glanced around the room, saw a poker game at one of the tables and saw that Amos Tarr was dealing. He studied his empty whiskey glass, trying to find the best way to say what he wanted to say. "You know the sheriff thinks I might have killed Old Levi."

"Yeah, I know."

"I guess you don't agree with him, or you wouldn't be drinking with me."

"Aw, old Harv's all right. He gets some strange ideas sometimes, that's all."

"There's something that worries me, I—"

An ear-splitting blast cut him off in mid-sentence.

The blast seemed to shake the room, in fact the whole world. It stunned the crowd inside The Palace, and for a moment everyone was silent.

Then a miner yelled, "Dynamite," and everyone moved at once.

Chapter Twenty-Three

Crystal Lee was satisfied when she saw the hotel manager put her money in his safe, along with the bags of gold, lock the door and put the key in his pocket. "It will be perfectly safe there, Miss Brown. Now if you'll excuse me I have some paperwork to attend to in my office." He went upstairs.

Only two other people were in the hotel lobby: two well-dressed men who appeared to be salesmen. They nodded politely as Crystal Lee turned to leave.

Crystal Lee's satisfaction froze in her throat when she saw the three men in the doorway.

They wore masks and held pistols in their hands.

"Don't move," one of them yelled. "One move and we start shooting."

No one moved. Crystal Lee froze in her tracks, horrified. The two drummers put their hands in the air without being ordered to and stood perfectly still.

"Where's the manager?"

No one answered.

"Tell me, goddammit, or I'll blow a hole in you." The

man with a red bandanna around his face shoved his pistol barrel up under the nose of one of the drummers.

"Upstairs," the man answered hurriedly.

"Where upstairs?"

The drummer answered with a weak voice, "I don't know, honest I don't."

"Never mind the manager," said another man, a man with a black muffler around his face. "We'll blow 'er open." He produced two sticks of dynamite already wired with a short fuse. Moving quickly, two masked men pulled the safe away from the wall, grunting with the effort. "Where'll we put 'er?" one of them asked.

"Under it. The bottom's the weakest part."

He struck a match and held it a moment as he looked around the room. "Ever'body take cover but don't go near the door." The two drummers squatted behind heavy wooden chairs. Crystal Lee ducked behind a velvet-covered sofa. The fuse was lit.

McCrea pushed his way through the crowd of miners to the door of The Palace and worked his way outside. He knew what had happened even before someone shouted in his ear. "The hotel. The safe. Someone blew up the safe."

Everyone was running toward the hotel. McCrea saw three masked men carrying canvas bags come out, stop suddenly at the sight of the crowd, fire two shots and duck back inside. A miner in front of the crowd dropped in his tracks.

The crowd stopped. The sheriff came running up and stopped. McCrea stopped. No one knew what to do. The crowd milled. Then the deputy, remembering that he was a legal authority, shouted, "Joe, you, some of you with guns, get around back. Don't let 'em out the back door."

A half-dozen men ran to the alley behind the hotel, drawing their pistols as they ran.

"All right." Sheriff G.B. Harvey took charge then. "They're bottled up in there. We've got the upper hand." He scanned the crowd. Every man who had a gun held it in his hand. Two others left, running, yelling that they were going to get their guns and come back.

The cold wind blew and the snow was getting heavier.

Again, the crowd was silent. Someone asked, "What're we gonna do?"

"Take this wounded man and take care of him the best you can," the sheriff ordered. "The rest of you with weapons, spread out."

When the hotel door opened, a dozen guns came up sharply, aimed at the door. But it was two well-dressed drummers who came out with their hands up. "Don't shoot. For God's sake, don't shoot." The guns were lowered.

"Who are you?" the sheriff demanded.

"I'm a representative of Taylor and Burns," one of them answered hastily. "We just happened to be in the hotel when they came in."

"Who else is in there?"

"They've got a woman." The drummer's voice was excited, and he spoke rapidly. "They said to tell you they'll kill her if you don't let them get away."

McCrea's blood suddenly turned cold. Icy fingers gripped his heart and ran up and down his back. Crystal.

"They said to tell you they want to get to their horses, and they're going to take the woman with them, and if anybody follows them they'll kill her."

"Crystal." The name came out of McCrea's throat as his stomach churned. He started walking to the hotel door.

"Wait a minute, McCrea," the deputy yelled. "Don't do anything foolish."

McCrea didn't answer. He was through talking.

Jaws clamped shut, McCrea walked. Anger boiled within him. His heart raced. He had done this before back home. His steps quickened. He had the .44 in his hand, the hammer back. He felt a terrible urge to run to the door and shoot as fast as he could cock the hammer and pull the trigger.

But then, as before, a coolness swept over him. There was no hurry. He walked slowly but surely along the boardwalk until he was even with the hotel door. A dozen lamps had the hotel lobby well lighted. The door was open.

McCrea stopped in front of the door.

One of the masked men held Crystal Lee around the waist in front of him. He fired first, but her struggles spoiled his aim. The other two men started shooting.

A bullet whistled past McCrea's left ear. Another tugged at his shirt sleeve. He brought the .44 up fast and sure and aimed.

His first shot hit the nearest man squarely in the chest, knocking him backward. The man's gun fired a shot into the ceiling as he fell.

Two more shots boomed. Splinters flew off the doorjamb. McCrea's hat was knocked off.

The second shot from McCrea's .44 sent another man falling sideways, blood gushing from a gaping wound in his throat.

Crystal Lee kicked back, bent her knees, jumped, and

finally broke free. She screamed, "Johnny."

McCrea had the hammer back. A bullet from the masked man's gun grazed the gun holster on his left hip. McCrea fired.

"Johnny." She rushed into his arms, weeping.

Three men were down, dead or dying. McCrea calmly holstered his gun and took Crystal Lee in his arms.

"Johnny. Thank God." She wept openly on his shoulder.

The crowd surged forward and surrounded them.

"Lord almighty," a man said. "If I didn't see it I wouldn't believe it."

"I still can't believe it," said another. "One against three and they saw him comin'."

"Hell," said another, speaking with authority. "I believe it. Hell, that's Johnny McCrea. I heard about him."

A man in bib overalls, a corncob pipe stuck in his mouth, pushed his way through the crowd and stood beside McCrea. "Now I know how it happened down there in the New Mexico Territory," said Arkansas Henessy. "I heered about that, too. Johnny here is the coolest, calmest man I ever seen in a fight." He looked around and saw that he had everyone's attention.

"An old lawdog tole me once the winner in a gunfight is the man that takes aim. These fast-draw gunhands always miss with their first shots." The crowd gathered closer to hear what the drawling man from Arkansas was saying.

"That's the way it happened down south, ain't it Johnny?" He didn't expect an answer and he got none. "They saw you acomin' an' figgered they had ta shoot first, so they yanked their guns and jerked tha triggers, an' their slugs went ever'where but where they wanted 'em to."

The crowd was quiet, listening.

"An' Johnny here just stood his ground, paid no mind ta tha lead aflyin' aroun' 'im, took aim and knocked over all three of 'em."

Crystal Lee hugged McCrea's arm. Sheriff G.B. Harvey squatted beside the downed men and pulled their masks off one at a time. He stood back, shaking his head. "Now, how in bloody hell did they get away? My God, they must have killed Samuel, the man I left guarding them. Good God."

One of the men was short and lean with one leg shorter than the other. Another was husky, bull-necked. The third had a scar down the right side of his cheek.

Crystal Lee whispered, "It's them."

The bull-necked man was bleeding from a hole in his left side, but he was still alive. He mumbled something and tried to sit up. Sheriff G.B. Harvey drew his pearl-handled pistol and shot him in the face. The man fell back. Crystal Lee gasped and buried her face in McCrea's chest.

Harvey holstered his gun and ran his hands over the dead man's body, then stood up. "I guess I was mistaken but I could have sworn he was reaching for a hideout gun." He shook his head. "Well, we just saved the state the cost of a trial. Everyone's dead now. They killed Old Levi and kidnapped Miss Brown." He looked over at McCrea. "You and your lady friend can go as you please now."

McCrea spoke for the first time since he had walked out of the mob in the street. "No, it's not over yet."

"What are you saying?" The sheriff was incredulous.

"There's another." McCrea looked over the crowd.

"Who?"

"I don't know for sure, but there's a man I want to speak to."

"Where?"

"The last time I saw him he was in The Palace."

"Well, point him out."

McCrea tried to move away, but Crystal Lee held onto his arm. "Please, Johnny, let the sheriff take care of it. Please don't go." Tears filled her eyes. "You've done enough."

McCrea shook his head sadly. "It wouldn't work. I'm the only one who can pin it on him. I'll have to confront him."

"Please, Johnny, don't go." Crystal Lee wanted to throw herself at her man's feet and beg him to stay with her. She would just die if anything happened to him. She couldn't let him go.

He tugged gently on his arm, trying to pull free of her grasp.

But she had to let him go. He was determined to do what he had to do, and she had to let him. She released her hold and stood there crying silently as McCrea walked stiff legged toward The Palace saloon.

Sheriff G.B. Harvey walked up beside him. A dozen men followed a good distance behind.

Only one man stood at the bar in The Palace. The bartender had hurried out with the rest of the mob to see what was happening. The lone man stood tall, six-foot-six. He sipped brandy from a glass and eyed the sheriff and the cowboy walking toward him.

"Him?" Harvey asked.

No answer came from McCrea, and the sheriff was the

first to speak to the tall man. "I, uh, want to apologize in advance, Mr. Tarr, but Mr. McCrea here thinks you might have had something to do with what's been going on around here."

Amos Tarr's drinking hand paused halfway to his mouth. "What? What are you talking about?"

Harvey nudged McCrea. "Well, speak up. But I want to warn you, folks around here are pretty fond of Mr. Tarr. He's the man who is building a new hotel and saloon."

For a horrible moment, McCrea was unsure of himself. Just a few hours earlier he was feeling guilty about Amos Tarr. Then after thinking the whole thing through and fitting bits of facts and happenings together, he was convinced that Amos Tarr was not what he appeared to be.

Lordy, he hoped he was right. He had to be right.

"Mr. McCrea." Amos Tarr was smiling broadly. "If you have anything to say to me, say it."

McCrea forced himself to look the tall man in the eye. "I think you're a crook." His voice was not quite steady. He forced himself to speak up. "You're not going to finish the hotel and saloon. You're getting ready to leave town."

Instead of showing anger, the tall man threw his head back and laughed. "Come now. What are you talking about?"

Fixing his eyes on the tall man's eyes, McCrea continued. "You're one of the slickest con men in the West." He turned to the sheriff. "Have you ever seen him pay cash for a transaction of any size?"

Harvey pondered the question. "Well yes, he bought a bunch of lots around here and paid cash for them."

"Yeah, he probably did at that." McCrea looked back at Amos Tarr. "Sure, you had a little cash when you first came here, and you made some wise investments. You sold the lots for enough to get started building a hotel and saloon. But that only got you started. You paid for everything else with worthless paper."

The smile left Amos Tarr's face. "Now listen, this is getting ridiculous. Sheriff, why do you let this man prattle on like that?"

McCrea answered, "Because it makes sense. You had big plans. But first you had to have a gold mine, one of the best. You bought a worthless mine and salted it. And," McCrea said and turned to the sheriff, "I'm betting he bribed a mining engineer to put out a false report."

"Now this is getting serious," the tall man said, a deadly warning in his voice.

"Listen, young fella." The sheriff was no longer calling him Mr. McCrea. "You had better know what you are talking about. This town owes you something for what you did back there, but don't think you can get away with just anything."

McCrea was insistent. "Check on it. He's trying to set up a phony corporation and sell stock in his gold mine. Check on it and I'll bet he's offering stock in St. Louis."

"Of course I am," Amos Tarr blurted out. "Why not? It's a worthwhile venture."

"It's worthless. A man named Smith sold you that mine, and I have heard on good authority that he wouldn't be so stupid as to sell a good mine for the price you paid."

A murmur went through the crowd at McCrea's back. Amos Tarr's face hardened.

"He's been going around town buying more property,

but with notes, not cash. I'd be willing to bet he's planning to sell all his holdings here for cash and leave the country before you find out his paper is worthless."

"He shore is." Heads swiveled toward Arkansas Henessy. "That's exactly what he's adoin'."

The sheriff asked, "What makes you say that, Mr. Henessy?"

"He's offered ta sell me tha hotel and saloon, an' I agreed ta buy 'em, but not 'til after we get a lawyer ta draw up papers amakin' him responsible for his debts. An' I'll tell ya somethin' else. He's got a partner, a secret partner he had to get permission from. He didn't mean to, but he let that slip."

"That is a normal way of conducting business, Mr. Henessy. There is nothing dishonest about that." Amos Tarr was forcing himself to relax now. "I'll admit I'm not a hotel operator nor a saloon keeper. I'm an entrepreneur. I like to get a profitable project going, sell it and look for another project."

"Sounds logical," said Sheriff G.B. Harvey.

"But it proves he was planning to leave town," McCrea insisted. "He came here by chance, maybe to hunt elk as he said, and he saw the town was going to boom, and he saw there was no bank and no telegraph, and he saw an opoportunity. He offered to buy Old Levi's mine from me with one of his notes, and I'll bet he'd have turned right around and sold it for cash just before he left."

"All right, what has all this got to do with murder, young fella? Are you saying he killed Old Levi?"

McCrea's mind was racing. A new factor had been added.

"Well, speak up," the sheriff barked. "Or shut up."

"Whoa now, wait a minute, sheriff," McCrea said. "I

didn't accuse him of murder. All I'm saying is he's fleecing a lot of people, including some hard-working people in Bluebird. It was his partner who committed murder."

"Well then." A sneer crept into the sheriff's voice. "I suppose you know all about who that jasper is."

McCrea knew now. He wished he didn't have to say it, that someone else would say it. He glanced at the faces behind him, at the deputy named Bud. They were waiting.

"It's you, Mr. Harvey."

"What?" The sheriff was shouting now. "What in Billy hell are you saying?"

Another murmur went through the crowd, and an angry voice said, "You'd better watch your mouth, mister."

McCrea picked out the man who had spoken. It was the deputy. McCrea looked back at the sheriff and swallowed a lump in his throat.

"It figures. I thought it was Amos Tarr until I heard he had a partner. It has to be you." McCrea glanced around again and saw hostility on the faces of some of the men. But now he knew he was right. "Sure. A smart lawman would have been wise to Amos Tarr right from the beginning. You were wise. But you made a deal with him and kept quiet. By being a secret partner you could put all the blame on him if anything went sour."

McCrea's voice was getting hoarse. He wasn't used to talking so much. His face was warm, and he was nervous at being the center of attention. "Too many things point to you," he continued. "First, Old Levi was supposed to be a smart old gent. He wouldn't let anybody sneak up on him. But when he saw it was the sheriff, he put his gun down."

Everyone was listening to McCrea. Even the deputy was waiting to hear what he would say next.

"You had the gold fever, too. You said once you're going to retire as soon as an election can be held. You want to retire rich. And it would have been easy for you to get back to town ahead of me after you left Old Levi dying. I had to go back to the Diamond J wagons first. You said you were out prospecting."

The deputy was shaking his head. "That's just bull, mister. You're just tellin' tall tales."

"No," McCrea said, now talking to the deputy, "there's more. The sheriff made sure he was out of town when I was dragged on a rope out to Willow Creek and Miss Brown was kidnapped. He stayed away until he thought all the dirty work was done. And I never could figure out why he was trying so hard to pin the killing on me and why he didn't haul me up to San Lomah and keep me in jail.

"It was because he wanted me to run. Sure, if I'd run he could have convinced everybody I did it, and he'd be forever in the clear. When I didn't run, he got some men to try to force information out of me. Seems everybody in town believed I knew something about Old Levi's mine."

Another pause and McCrea had to clear his throat. "Old Levi tried to talk before he died but he couldn't. Once, when Miss Brown and I were up there near Squaw Mountain, I thought he'd tried to give me a clue when he tipped over his sack of sugar and pointed at it. I thought he was trying to say something about a snowslide. But now that I'm thinking about it again—his sugar was the Morning Star brand, and the sack had a picture of a big star on it. The old man was pointing at that star and trying to tell me it was the sheriff."

McCrea had to swallow again to moisten his throat. No one else said anything. McCrea could see that the crowd and the deputy were thinking about what he had said. But he had more to say.

"It was easy for him to get some help. He just had a talk with some of the prisoners in the county jail at San Lomah. He promised them wealth if they'd force me and Miss Brown to tell them what he thought Old Levi had told us. And he picked up his empty shell casings at the old man's camp, because if anybody saw them they would know they'd been fired from that fancy gun of his, probably one of those new Colt self-cocking thirty-eights. At first, I thought it was Amos Tarr who shot at me, but if he'd shot at me with his long gun I'd be dead. No, it had to be somebody armed with only a pistol. That's why it was so easy for me to drive him off when I got that Henry in my hands. And—"

McCrea had to stop again. His throat was tightening.

"Now see here, mister." It was Bud, the deputy, talking. "You've pointed out some reasons to be suspicious, but well, he's the sheriff and the governor trusts him."

"He's a political hack," McCrea said. "I've seen his kind before. He politicks for the governor, and the governor rewards him with a soft job, a political plum. This was once a soft job. If there was any work to be done, he just deputized some volunteers. Except, of course, when he was the guilty man."

"But," the deputy said, "he's always been a gentleman. He's no killer."

Shaking his head sadly, McCrea said, "He once accused me of being a good actor. He can act rings around me anytime. And if you don't think he can kill, just remember a few minutes ago when he shot a dying man. He was afraid that man would live long enough to point the finger at him."

It was the bearded man who spoke next. "Maybe you ought to arrest 'im, Bud. He's beginnin' to look guilty."

"Aw hell, I can't arrest the sheriff. Hell, I'm just a temporary deputy. I don't know nothin' about arrestin' nobody. Besides, I ain't right certain he's done anything wrong."

"Well I am." Amos Tarr had been forgotten. Now he stood close to G.B. Harvey and towered over him. "I'll admit I've flimflammed a few folks, but I've never tortured and murdered anybody. Look at this." Amos Tarr held out the nugget he had been showing off. "He loaned it to me to show to everyone as proof that the Badger Mine is rich. He loaned it to me the day after that old prospector was killed. It never occurred to me until now that he was involved in anything else, but—"

No one saw the gun appear in Sheriff G.B. Harvey's hand. The explosion of the .38 caliber cartridge made a deafening, hollow sound in the crowded room. Amos Tarr fell back against the bar. A red spot spread across the middle of his chest, ruining the flowery vest.

Without thinking, McCrea reached for the gun on his hip, but before he could draw it he found himself looking into the bore of the pistol in G.B. Harvey's hand.

McCrea froze. He had no chance. The sheriff's eyes were wild. His finger tightened on the trigger.

Another gun boomed, and G.B. Harvey dropped immediately. He was dead when he hit the floor. His head was swollen out of shape.

Amos Tarr stood drunkenly at the bar, the small house pistol in his hand. He smiled weakly at McCrea. "That's another one you owe me, Mr. McCrea. No hard feelings." His eyeballs rolled upward and he slowly collapsed like a balloon with the air hissing out.

McCrea caught him and eased him to the floor. "I'm sorry, Mr. Tarr. I really am." McCrea realized there was nothing more he could say.

He stood up and looked with dull eyes at the crowd. He moved toward the door, and the crowd parted to allow him through. Arkansas Henessy fell into step beside him as he reached the plank walk outside.

"I suspicioned Ol' Harv for a crook, but I didn't know he was a killer." He put a hand on McCrea's arm. "Looks like I'm agoin' ta own a big piece of the town of Bluebird. I'll buy Miss Brown's cafe, too. You tell 'er that, will ya?"

"Yeah, I'll tell her."

When the sound of gunshots reached Crystal Lee Brown, it was as if a painful electric shock went through her. "Oh no," she cried. "Oh please, God." She hurried toward the saloon, tripped over her long skirts, fell, got up and ran. She had to know. She had to see him.

She stopped when she saw two men come out of the saloon and walk toward her. One of them dropped back and the other continued toward her.

Crystal Lee Brown ran to him, hugged him and wept with relief.

John McCrea put an arm around her and together they walked, arms around each other, down the streets of Bluebird in the new state of Colorado, unmindful of the cold wind and blowing snow. Inside her cabin, they held each other tightly, not speaking. Finally, McCrea struck a match and lit the oil lamp. He took a dainty handkerchief from her dress pocket and gently wiped her eyes.

"Is it all over now, Johnny?"

"Yes, Crystal. It's over now. We're going home."

MORE OF THE HOTTEST WESTERNS!

GUNN #19: HIGH MOUNTAIN HUSSY (1348, $2.25)
by Jory Sherman

Gunn gets intimate with a dark-haired temptress—and she's revealing it all! Her father's been murdered, but not before writing a cryptic message that Gunn's obliged to decipher—before a killer deciphers Gunn!

GUNN #20: TEN-GALLON TEASE (1378, $2.25)
by Jory Sherman

With Apache raiders and a desperate outlaw gang each planning an ambush, Gunn's chance to make fast money selling California horses to the U.S. Cavalry looks slim. He's lucky he can count on the services of a wild and beautiful tomboy to help him in the clinches!

GUNN #21: SWEET TEXAS TART (1494, $2.25)
by Jory Sherman

Gunn's caught in the middle of a range war with ladies on either side wooing him. As the competition for his gun gets stiffer, Gunn's in a dangerous game as one of the ladies could be a man-eater!

SHELTER #19: THE HARD MEN (1428, $2.25)
by Paul Ledd

Shelter's aiming to cross another member of the death battalion off his hit list—except he's hunting the wrong man. Morgan's in for trouble, and it takes the hot touch of an eager squaw to get him ready for action!

SHELTER #20: SADDLE TRAMP (1465, $2.25)
by Paul Ledd

Tracking another killer, Shelter takes on the identity of a murdered U.S. marshal and lays down the law. And a buxom bargirl named Lola likes the way the law lays!

SHELTER #21: SHOTGUN SUGAR (1547, $2.25)
by Paul Ledd

Itching for revenge, Shelter picks up the trail of his cattle-rustling enemy Julian Cruz and dogs his steps north to Wyoming. A beautiful outlaw in distress, Annie, has her own score to settle with Cruz, but when it comes to Shelter, she thirsts for more than blood!

Available wherever paperbacks are sold, or order direct from the Publisher. Send cover price plus 50¢ per copy for mailing and handling to Zebra Books, Dept. 1635, 475 Park Avenue South, New York, N.Y. 10016. DO NOT SEND CASH.

THE NEWEST ADVENTURES AND ESCAPADES OF BOLT
by Cort Martin

#11: THE LAST BORDELLO (1224, $2.25)

A working girl in Angel's camp doesn't stand a chance — unless Jared Bolt takes up arms to bring a little peace to the town . . . and discovers that the trouble is caused by a woman who used to do the same!

#12: THE HANGTOWN HARLOTS (1274, $2.25)

When the miners come to town, the local girls are used to having wild parties, but events are turning ugly . . . and murderous. Jared Bolt knows the trade of tricking better than anyone, though, and is always the first to come to a lady in need . . .

#13: MONTANA MISTRESS (1316, $2.25)

Roland Cameron owns the local bank, the sheriff, and the town — and he thinks he owns the sensuous saloon singer, Charity, as well. But the moment Bolt and Charity eye each other there's fire — especially gunfire!

#14: VIRGINIA CITY VIRGIN (1360, $2.25)

When Katie's bawdy house holds a high stakes raffle, Bolt figures to take a chance. It's winner take all — and the prize is a budding nineteen year old virgin! But there's a passle of gun-toting folks who'd rather see Bolt in a coffin than in the virgin's bed!

#15: BORDELLO BACKSHOOTER (1411, $2.25)

Nobody has ever seen the face of curvaceous Cherry Bonner, the mysterious madam of the bawdiest bordello in Cheyenne. When Bolt keeps a pimp with big ideas and a terrible temper from having his way with Cherry, gunfire flares and a gambling man would bet on murder: Bolt's!

#16: HARDCASE HUSSY (1513, $2.25)

Traveling to set up his next bordello, Bolt is surrounded by six prime ladies of the evening. But just as Bolt is about to explore this lovely terrain, their stagecoach is ambushed by the murdering Beeler gang, bucking to be in Bolt's position!

Available wherever paperbacks are sold, or order direct from the Publisher. Send cover price plus 50¢ per copy for mailing and handling to Zebra Books, Dept. 1635, 475 Park Avenue South, New York, N.Y. 10016. DO NOT SEND CASH.

FORGE AHEAD IN THE SCOUT SERIES
BY BUCK GENTRY

#12: YELLOWSTONE KILL (1254, $2.50)
The Scout is tracking a warband that kidnapped some young and lovely ladies. And there's danger at every bend in the trail as Holten closes in, but the thought of all those women keeps the Scout riding hard!

#13: OGLALA OUTBREAK (1287, $2.50)
When the Scout's long time friend, an Oglala chief, is murdered, Holten vows to avenge his death. But there's a young squaw whose appreciation for what he's trying to do leads him down an exciting trail of her own!

#14: CATHOUSE CANYON (1345, $2.50)
Enlisting the aid of his Oglala friends, the Scout plans to blast a band of rampaging outlaws to hell — and hopes to find a little bit of heaven in the arms of his sumptuous companion . . .

#15: TEXAS TEASE (1392, $2.50)
Aiding the Texas Rangers, with the luscious Louise on one side and the warring Kiowa-Apache on the other, Eli's apt to find himself coming and going at exactly the same time!

#16: VIRGIN OUTPOST (1445, $2.50)
Tracking some murdering raiders, the Scout uncovers a luscious survivor, a hot-blooded vixen widowed on her wedding night. He'll try his hardest to please her between the sheets — before the raiders nail him between the eyes!

#17: BREAKNECK BAWDYHOUSE (1514, $2.50)
When a vicious gang of gunslingers sets up a hardcase haven — complete with three cathouses — the Scout knows the Sioux plan a massacre. Rescuing the ladies of the evening, the Scout finds it hard when he tries to convince them he came for business, not pleasure!

Available wherever paperbacks are sold, or order direct from the Publisher. Send cover price plus 50¢ per copy for mailing and handling to Zebra Books, Dept. 1635, 475 Park Avenue South, New York, N.Y. 10016. DO NOT SEND CASH.

DON'T MISS THESE EXCITING BESTSELLERS
by Lewis Orde

EAGLES (1500, $3.95)
Never forgetting his bitter childhood as an orphan, Roland Eagles survived by instinct alone. From the horrors of London under siege to the splendors of New York high society, he would ruthlessly take what he desired—in business, and in bed—never foreseeing how easily his triumphs could turn into tragedy.

MUNICH 10 (1300, $3.95)
They've killed her lover, and they've kidnapped her son. Now the world-famous actress is swept into a maelstrom of international intrigue and bone-chilling suspense—and the only man who can help her pursue her enemies is a complete stranger . . .

HERITAGE (1100, $3.75)
Beautiful innocent Leah and her two brothers were forced by the holocaust to flee their parents' home. A courageous immigrant family, each battled for love, power and their very lifeline—their HERITAGE.

THE LION'S WAY (900, $3.75)
An all-consuming saga that spans four generations in the life of troubled and talented David, who struggles to rise above his immigrant heritage and rise to a world of glamour, fame and success!

DEADFALL (1400, $3.95)
by Lewis Orde and Bill Michaels
The two men Linda cares about most, her father and her lover, entangle her in a plot to hold Manhattan Island hostage for a billion dollars ransom. When the bridges and tunnels to Manhattan are blown, Linda is suddenly a terrorist—except *she's* the one who's terrified!

Available wherever paperbacks are sold, or order direct from the Publisher. Send cover price plus 50¢ per copy for mailing and handling to Zebra Books, Dept. 1635, 475 Park Avenue South, New York, N.Y. 10016. DO NOT SEND CASH.